Imagination According to Humphrey

Betty G. Birney

ff

FABER & FABER

This edition first published in 2015
by Faber and Faber Limited
Bloomsbury House, 74–77
Great Russell Street, London WC1B 3DA

Typeset by Faber & Faber Ltd
Printed and bound by CPI Group (UK) Ltd, Croydon CR0 4YY

A CIP record for this book
is available from the British Library

ISBN 978–0–571–28251–7

FSC
www.fsc.org
MIX
Paper from
responsible sources
FSC® C101712

2 4 6 8 10 9 7 5 3 1

To my parents and teachers who
encouraged my imagination to soar –
and to all the teachers and parents who
are doing the same thing today!

Contents

Imagine This!

The golden dragon bent his head low and Gil Goodfriend crawled up his neck. When the dragon lifted his head, Gil was higher than Tower Peak, which was the tallest mountain in the kingdom.

It was after lunch and our teacher, Mrs Brisbane, was reading a book to everyone in Room 26 of Longfellow School, where I live.

She continued:

'Hold on,' the dragon said. 'We're going up.'

Suddenly, Gil and the dragon rose high above his village. Wind whipped through his hair. It was thrilling until the dragon suddenly veered to the right and swooped down low, grazing ten treetops with his majestic, fire-tipped wings. One treetop caught fire, but luckily, the wind blew the fire out.

Someone in the back of the room gasped. Mrs Brisbane kept on reading.

'Are you all right?' the dragon called to Gil. Surprisingly, he was perfectly fine.

He was perfectly fine? My whiskers wiggled at the thought of flying over fiery treetops.

Gil peered down as they soared above his house. It looked no bigger than a toy. In seconds, the whole village of Bumpshire looked like tiny dots on a white background, even though it was July.

You see, Gil's village had really terrible weather. It snowed in the summer and it flooded in the winter and they had BIG-BIG-BIG storms all the time. It was miserable, but no one knew how to make it better.

'Only you can change the weather back to normal,' the dragon said.

'I'm just a boy,' Gil said. 'Why me?'

'Yes, WHY-WHY-WHY?' I squeaked.

The dragon didn't answer.

After a few moments, Gil shouted, 'Am I ever coming back?'

The dragon's voice boomed, 'That depends on you and you alone!'

Mrs Brisbane looked up at all of my classmates.

My tail twitched as I imagined riding a dragon. Dogs are smaller than dragons but they're still pretty scary and have bad breath. At least they don't breathe fire!

'Don't stop!' Slow-Down-Simon shouted.

Mrs Brisbane closed the book. 'I'm sorry, but I have to keep you in suspense until tomorrow.'

Calm-Down-Cassie shivered. 'The dragon seems nice, but I hope I never meet a real one!'

'I agree!' I said.

Of course, since I'm a small classroom hamster, all that my human friends heard was 'Squeak.'

'BOING-BOING!' My neighbour Og jumped up and down in his tank. He's the classroom frog. Maybe he's afraid of dragons, too.

'Dragons aren't real,' Tell-the-Truth-Thomas said. 'They're only in books. You shouldn't believe everything you read in a story.'

'There *are* real dragons,' Not-Now-Nicole said.

'Eeek!' I squeaked.

Thomas laughed. 'You have a really good imagination!'

'But there were dragons a long time ago,' Cassie said. 'Right, Mrs Brisbane?'

Mrs Brisbane smiled. 'Some stories are true. They're called non-fiction. But other stories come out of the imagination. Those books are called fiction, like this book.'

'There are dragons that aren't imaginary,' Nicole said. 'My brother has one.'

'Really?' Mrs Brisbane asked.

'Really!' Nicole said.

Stop-Talking-Sophie raised her hand. 'I don't see any dragons walking around today – but that doesn't mean they never did. Why did so many people write stories about them?'

'That's a good question,' Mrs Brisbane said. 'Any ideas on why people might have imagined there were dragons?'

The room was quiet for a moment.

I had no ideas at all. I would NEVER-NEVER-NEVER want to imagine there were real scary dragons!

Just-Joey raised his hand. 'Maybe people saw some big old bones – like dinosaur bones – and thought they were from something like a dragon. And maybe there was a forest fire and people thought the beast breathed flames that started the fire.'

'Yes!' Thomas said. 'And then they started to imagine all kinds of things the dragon did.'

Mrs Brisbane nodded. 'I think it might have happened like that.'

I still wasn't sure.

The room was quiet until Not-Now-Nicole giggled. 'Maybe we should get a dragon for a classroom pet. One like my brother's.'

It had been hard enough to get used to a frog as the other pet in Room 26. Especially a frog like Og, who makes a weird sound and has some odd habits. But a fire-breathing dragon?

'NO-NO-NO!' I squeaked.

The students sitting close to our table heard me and laughed.

'Don't worry, Humphrey,' Thomas said. 'We're not getting a dragon . . . because they're imaginary.'

By that time, I wasn't even interested in an *imaginary* dragon.

'Tell us about this dragon your brother has, Nicole,' Mrs Brisbane said.

'Her name is Pearl and she's really beautiful,' Nicole said.

My classmates burst out laughing.

I didn't think what Nicole said was funny at all. She looked REALLY-REALLY-REALLY upset.

'She is *too* real! I'll prove it to you,' she said. 'I'll call my mum right now. She'll tell you.'

'Not-Now-Nicole,' Mrs Brisbane said. 'It's time for us to get out our maths books. You can explain later.'

I usually try to learn along with my fellow classmates, even though I don't have a maths book. But my eyelids got heavy and I slipped into my sleeping hut for a short nap.

When I woke up, I crawled back out and glanced across the table by the window where my cage sits.

Og was in his tank next to my cage. I think he was dozing, too, but it's hard to tell. Sometimes he closes his eyes but he's not sleeping.

(I told you, he's a little odd.)

I glanced out of the other side of my cage and was unsqueakably happy to see that there was no pet dragon blowing hot smoke at me. Whew!

Then I looked towards the front of the room.

I don't know how long I'd slept, but instead of writing numbers on the board, Mrs Brisbane was talking about writing.

'This is my favourite time in the school year,' she said. 'Today, we start being writers. I know you all brought your writing notebooks today. Will you hold them up?'

The other students all held up notebooks and each one was different.

Helpful-Holly's had big yellow sunflowers on it.

Tall-Paul's had a motorcycle on the cover, while Small-Paul's had a photo of the space shuttle.

I climbed up to the tippy-top of my cage so I could see better. I saw smiley faces, princesses, polka dots and stars.

My friends in Room 26 have a lot of interests!

'Once you start writing your ideas in your notebooks, you're on your way to being a writer,' Mrs Brisbane explained.

'What if we don't have any ideas?' Hurry-Up-Harry asked.

Some of my classmates giggled.

'I mean, what if we don't have any ideas about what to write?' Harry said.

'We all have ideas,' Mrs Brisbane said. 'The notebook is a tool to help you.'

'Like a hammer?' Fix-It-Felipe asked. I know he likes hammers, because he can fix just about anything.

More of my friends giggled.

Mrs Brisbane laughed, too. 'In a way, yes. It's a tool to help you learn how to find ideas and develop them.'

Helpful-Holly laughed. 'I think Felipe would rather have a hammer.'

'All right, enough joking, class,' our teacher said. 'To get you started, I'm going to give you an assignment.' She paused to write on the board.

If I could fly, I would fly like a _____

'And then fill in the blank however you like,' she explained. 'You can start now, but the bell will ring soon, so bring in your completed work tomorrow.'

'Fly? Without a plane?' Cassie asked.

'You get to decide if it's a plane or a bird or anything you can imagine,' Mrs Brisbane said. 'Then I want you to write a sentence saying where you would go. This is the beginning of your assignment and eventually you will end up with a real story.'

She pointed to her head. 'Use your imaginations. And spend some time thinking about your idea before you start writing.'

I heard some sighs and dropped pencils as my friends opened their notebooks.

Hurry-Up-Harry looked confused.

Slow-Down-Simon looked grumpy.

Calm-Down-Cassie looked anything but calm.

After they wrote down the beginning that Mrs Brisbane assigned, they stopped writing. They just stared at the blank pages.

'Do we have to decide now?' Do-It-Now-Daniel asked.

'Start thinking now,' Mrs Brisbane said. 'You'll share your ideas tomorrow.'

Just-Joey shook his head. 'I never know how to start.'

Mrs Brisbane said, 'It sometimes helps if you brainstorm.'

Eeek! Brainstorm? My ears wiggled at the word. Imagine having rain and lightning and thunder in your brain!

'Take five minutes and write down any idea that comes into your head,' our teacher explained. 'Even if the idea seems silly or impossible, or if you don't even like it, write it down anyway. *No rubbing out.* When the five minutes is up, look at your list of ideas and you'll probably find at least one that you would like to write about. Then you can start. The assignment is only two sentences.'

'How long do the sentences have to be?' Sophie asked. 'Because sometimes a sentence is long and sometimes a sentence is short and sometimes—'

Sophie didn't get to finish because the bell rang and the notebooks were quickly closed.

Most of my friends dashed for their backpacks and coats, but Sophie headed straight for Mrs Brisbane.

'I dream about flying all the time,' she said. 'Once I dreamed I flew to this island and all my friends there were parrots, but they could talk and I could understand them because parrots can talk. Oh, and you know what? Once . . .'

Mrs Brisbane glanced at the clock. 'Why don't you write about it, Sophie? I don't want you to miss your bus home.'

Sophie looked disappointed. 'I'd rather talk about it than write about it.'

'I know,' Mrs Brisbane said. 'But you'll learn.'

She pointed Sophie in the direction of the cloakroom.

While my friends dashed out of Room 26, Mrs Brisbane cleaned the board and neatly stacked the papers on her desk.

When she had her coat on and was ready to leave, she came over to the table. 'Goodnight,

Humphrey and Og. I'll see you tomorrow.'

After she left, I watched out the window and waited until all the cars and buses were gone for the day.

Then I turned towards Og's tank. 'Do you think dragons are real? Because to squeak the truth, I'm not sure.'

Og was silent.

It's HARD-HARD-HARD to know what a frog thinks about. For one thing, Og always has a goofy grin on his face. And if he does talk, he sounds more like a broken guitar string than a sensible animal like a hamster.

This time, he didn't even say 'BOING!' He just dived into the water side of his tank and began splashing.

I looked out the window again. It was getting dark.

I had something important to do, but I had to wait.

The big clock on the wall doesn't make any noise during the day, but it makes a lot of noise at night. TICK-TICK-TICK. Even an odd frog is better company than that. I waited for the other sound and finally it came.

RATTLE-RATTLE-RATTLE.

Then the turn of the doorknob and the click of the switch. The room filled with light.

Aldo had arrived!

Aldo came every night during the week to clean Room 26 and all the rooms in Longfellow School.

'Hello, my friends,' he said cheerily. 'I hope you're both well.'

'I am, Aldo. How are you?' I squeaked as I rushed to the front of my cage to greet him.

'BOING-BOING!' Og said.

'I am well,' Aldo said with a smile. 'Thank you for asking.'

He went straight to work, sweeping, dusting, mopping, and emptying the bin.

On most nights, Aldo first stops to talk or even do a trick, like balancing his broom on one finger.

But tonight, he didn't stop at all.

'I need to get home to study,' Aldo said. 'The quicker I get out of here, the sooner I can study. And the quicker I get out of college, the sooner I can start teaching. After all, I'm about to be a dad.'

I already knew Aldo had gone back to college to learn to be a teacher, and I knew he and his wife, Maria, were going to be parents. Of twins!

Aldo worked so fast, he was almost a blur.

I was unsqueakably happy when he sat down to eat dinner with us.

I was even happier when he pulled out a small piece of carrot for me.

And Og seemed pleased when he threw some Froggy Fish Sticks in his tank.

Aldo ate his sandwich almost as fast as he'd swept the floors.

'Wish me luck, fellows,' he said as he got up to leave. 'I have a really big test tomorrow.'

'Good luck, Aldo!' I called out to him as he turned off the lights.

'BOING!' Og said.

The light from street lamps streamed through the window and gave my cage a nice glow.

Once I saw Aldo's car pull out of the car park, I quickly went to work.

I'd been waiting hours for this moment.

My friends weren't the only students with

notebooks. I have one, too. I keep it hidden behind the little mirror in my cage.

It's a hamster-sized notebook that was a present from Ms Mac, a teacher I love as much as I love Mrs Brisbane. There's a tiny pencil, too.

My notebook doesn't have flowers or footballs on the cover. In fact, it's pretty plain.

But it's VERY-VERY-VERY special to me, because I write all my secret thoughts in it.

My notebook is like an old friend, and I couldn't wait to get to work.

I opened it and began to think. If I could fly wherever I wanted, where would I go?

There are a lot of places where hamsters like me can't go. We can't go on aeroplanes or field trips or to football games or restaurants.

But there are some places we can go that humans can't – tiny places like between the cracks in the floorboards or inside a little hamster ball.

If I could fly, I would fly like a . . . what?

I wrote in my notebook almost every night, but suddenly I couldn't think of a thing to say.

'Use your imagination,' Mrs Brisbane had said.

'Where are you, imagination?' I squeaked. 'Did you fly away?'

But all I heard back was silence. There was nothing like lightning or thunder in my brain!

I was wide awake, but my imagination had gone to sleep.

'Og, where would you go if you could fly?' I squeaked.

'BOING-BOING-BOING!' Og jumped up and down excitedly.

I realized my mistake.

The word 'fly' means something special to frogs, because 'flies' are things they like to *eat*.

My tummy did a flip-flop just thinking about *that*.

'Never mind,' I told him.

I started thinking about things that fly, like birds, aeroplanes, rockets . . . and flies.

Aeroplanes and rockets are huge and noisy things that go way above the clouds and who knows where?

Birds are squawky creatures with sharp beaks, although it would be nice to fly anywhere I wanted to go.

And I wouldn't want to be the kind of fly

that ends up in a frog's mouth.

The problem is, I'm HAPPY-HAPPY-HAPPY living in my cage in Room 26 and seeing my human friends every day. I really like helping my friends.

I stared and stared at that blank page and I guess I dozed off, because the next thing I knew, sunshine was streaming through the window and Mrs Brisbane was jiggling her key in the door.

I barely had time to push my notebook and pencil behind the mirror before I heard her say, 'Morning!'

My Writer's Ramblings

I have so many great ideas
All through the day,
But when it's time to write
    them down,
Poof! They've flown away.

Imagine That!

As soon as class began, Nicole raised her hand. 'Mrs Brisbane, I brought a picture of my brother's dragon,' she said. 'Can I pass it around?'

'Not-Now-Nicole,' Mrs Brisbane said. 'We'll all look at it later. But first, we have our spelling test.'

Lots of my friends groaned.

I groaned, too.

I was curious to find out if my friends' imaginations had come up with great ideas. Mine certainly hadn't!

I was thinking so much about the writing assignment, I missed several words on our test. It turns out that the word 'require' does not have a 'k' in it.

And I don't know what I was thinking when I spelled 'polite' this way: poo-lite.

After the test, Nicole raised her hand again. 'Now can I show you Pearl?' she asked.

Mrs Brisbane said she could. Nicole took a picture out of her desk and passed it around.

I climbed up my tree branch to see my classmates' reactions.

Slow-Down-Simon's eyes got wide as he looked at the picture. 'Amazing!'

Sophie made a face and shivered as she passed the photo to Holly. 'Eww! That's horrible,' she said. 'That can't be real!'

Thomas laughed when he saw the photo. 'Now I get it. That's a real dragon, all right!'

'I want one of those!' Just-Joey exclaimed.

Cassie looked terrified as she gazed at the photo. 'That's awful! How big is it? Does it breathe fire?'

Nicole giggled. 'No. It's not real big, but it's a lot bigger than Humphrey. And Og!'

'Eeek! I squeaked.

'*I* think she's beautiful,' Rolling-Rosie said.

Was Pearl beautiful or horrible? I wished I

could get a look at that picture. Or maybe I was glad I couldn't see it.

Mrs Brisbane smiled as she looked at the photo. 'Pearl is lovely,' she said. 'When we have more time, you can tell us all about her.'

'She's a bearded dragon and she's—' Nicole began.

'Eeek!' I squeaked. It slipped out because I had never heard of a *girl* with a beard – not even a girl dragon!

'Not-Now-Nicole,' Mrs Brisbane said. 'We need to work on our writing. But I will make sure to give you time later. Right now, I want you all to open your notebooks.'

I didn't actually open mine, because it's a secret. Besides, there was no point since I hadn't written *one word*.

But I REALLY-REALLY-REALLY wanted to hear what my friends had come up with.

'So, who wants to share what you wrote?' Mrs Brisbane asked.

Lots of hands went up! Mrs Brisbane called on Do-It-Now-Daniel.

'If I could, I'd fly like a helicopter. I'd head straight to my house, land in the front garden, and go back to bed,' he said.

Everybody laughed – even our teacher.

'I would fly like a kite to go to Winfield to see Phoebe,' Helpful-Holly read. 'If I could fly, I could see her any time I wanted.'

Holly really missed Phoebe, who had recently moved away.

I missed her, too. I looked over at the place where she used to sit and so did Holly.

'I had a hard time deciding which idea to use,' Thomas read. 'But here's what I finally wrote: If I could fly, I would soar like an eagle. I'd like to go to Egypt and see the Pyramids.'

We'd just finished studying ancient Egypt and I thought I'd like to see them, too.

Rolling-Rosie's hand waved back and forth.

'Tell me, Rosie, where would you fly?' Mrs Brisbane asked.

'I'd fly out of my wheelchair, straight up to the sky and I'd keep flying all over the world, just like a bird!' Her eyes glowed with excitement.

'Where would you go first?' Mrs Brisbane asked.

Rosie thought for a few seconds. 'I think I'd like to see those Pyramids, too.'

Everyone's ideas were so exciting! Just-Joey wanted to fly like a hawk to Africa, and Small-Paul wanted to fly to outer space. That's a LONG-LONG-LONG way to fly!

Simon wanted to fly like a dragon to Italy because he likes Italian food. 'Especially pizza!' he said. 'I could use my fire-breathing to heat it up.'

The whole class chuckled at that, including me!

Kelsey wanted to fly like a butterfly to any place she could see a professional ballet.

'I'm happy to see that your imaginations are working very well,' Mrs Brisbane said. 'Now I want you to continue the paragraph, describing exactly what you'd like to see on your trip and telling us why.'

There was a groan from the back of the room.

I imagined the groan was from Daniel, wishing he could helicopter back to bed.

'You can start now,' Mrs Brisbane said. 'The paragraph is due tomorrow.'

Some of my friends started scribbling in their notebooks right away.

Others, like Kelsey and Joey, chewed on their pencils and stared at the blank pages.

Believe me, I knew how they felt!

Sophie turned to Nicole. 'Do you think you'd have wings like a bird or more like a plane? Even with wings, I don't see how a plane flies, because it's so heavy. Or maybe wings like a butterfly. I might change my mind . . .'

'Please Stop-Talking-Sophie,' Mrs Brisbane said. 'Believe me, there's no way to talk and write at the same time.'

Sophie looked embarrassed. 'Sorry.'

Later, after my friends came back from afternoon break, Mrs Brisbane asked Nicole to tell us more about Pearl.

'We call her Pearl because her eyes are like shiny black pearls,' she said.

'*I* think it's a lizard,' Thomas said.

Nicole looked frustrated. 'It's called a bearded *dragon*. Some people call them "beardies".'

'Which is a type of lizard,' Thomas said.

Thomas knows a lot because he reads so many books.

'Bearded dragons come from Australia and they're really nice,' Nicole said. 'And pretty, too.'

That might be true, but I wondered how BIG Pearl was.

Mrs Brisbane thanked her and then came the BEST-BEST-BEST part of the day. She read to us from the dragon book.

Gil Goodfriend and the dragon landed up on a cloud where there was a whole village of dragons. The houses were all made of stone. Gil thought they were pretty clever not to build wooden houses as they would burn easily. The houses were huge and had fire-breathing chimneys. The great castle had a moat around it with water to put out fires. And the streets were made of shiny dragon scales.

I thought clouds were pretty, fluffy things. I never thought about fire-breathing dragons living up there!

It turns out that these were nice dragons who made it rain so the flowers would grow and also produced rainbows. (Bumpshire, however, didn't get a lot of rainbows.)

But on another cloud there were some *very bad* dragons. They made thunder, lightning, blizzards, sleet and hail. Even *tornadoes*. They were the reason that it snowed in the summer in Bumpshire.

Mrs Brisbane read:

'Please help us, Gil,' Goldie pleaded.

The golden dragon was named Goldie – I forgot to tell you that – sorry!

'I'm not sure what I can do, but the people in Bumpshire would be very happy if I could help, too,' Gil said. 'Just one day nice enough for a picnic would make us happy.'

'You can help us figure out how to defeat them,' Goldie said. 'And believe me, the whole kingdom will be grateful to you.'

I tell you, that story was brilliant!

I guess it wasn't true, but the way Mrs Brisbane read it made it seem true.

And I couldn't wait to find out what happened next!

Unfortunately, the bell rang all too quickly and school was over for the day.

On his way out of the room, Small-Paul asked Mrs Brisbane where she would fly if she could.

'That's easy,' she said. 'I'd fly like the wind to Tokyo and visit my son Jason and his wife. Of course, I could take a plane, but I'd love to see all the sights on the way there.'

After my friends had left for the day, Mrs Brisbane let out a huge sigh. 'Jason is just so far away,' she said.

She looked a little sad.

I don't like to see Mrs Brisbane looking sad.

'If I could fly, I'd take you there!' I squeaked.

'BOING-BOING!' Og chimed in.

I was sorry that I'd imagined he only thought about eating flies. He cares about Mrs Brisbane as much as I do!

Mrs Brisbane put on her coat. 'What am I complaining about? Jason is so happy. And we're saving up for a trip to Japan this summer.'

'GREAT-GREAT-GREAT!' I squeaked.

'BOING!' Og agreed.

Mrs Brisbane walked over to the table where

my cage and Og's tank sit. 'I can always count on you two to cheer me up.'

'Yes, you can!' I replied.

And I'm happy to say, Mrs Brisbane was smiling as she left Room 26 for the night.

•ö•

'I think I did pretty well in my test,' Aldo announced when he came in to clean that night.

Then he yawned. 'I didn't get much sleep, though. I guess I'll have to get used to that once the twins are born.'

Aldo yawned a lot as he cleaned, but he still did a good job.

When he had finished, he pulled a chair up to the table and faced Og and me as he ate his dinner.

'You two are lucky to have each other for company,' he told us. 'That guinea pig in Ms Mac's room must get a little lonely.'

'Gigi?' I asked.

'I think her name is Gigi,' Aldo said. 'Something like that.'

Ms Mac was the wonderful teacher who

first brought me to Room 26. Now she was teaching in a different classroom.

I'd been a little upset when she got her class a guinea pig, but she'd told me I'd always be her favourite pet. I believe her, too. Ms Mac would NEVER-NEVER-NEVER lie.

'Too bad you can't visit her,' he said.

Aldo's smart but he doesn't know everything For one thing, he doesn't know about the lock-that-doesn't-lock on my cage – and I hope he never finds out!

He stood up and yawned again.

'Time to move on, fellows,' he said as he pushed his cleaning cart towards the door. 'Goodnight!'

'Goodnight, Aldo!' I squeaked. 'Get some sleep!'

'BOING-BOING!' Og chimed in.

Once he was gone and Room 26 was quiet, I took out my little notebook and tried again.

If my friends could come up with great ideas using their imaginations, so could I!

I tried to imagine myself flying.

I looked at myself in the little mirror and tried to picture myself with wings. I think I'd look pretty silly!

Then I stared hard at the blank page.

It was REALLY-REALLY-REALLY blank.

What was it Mrs Brisbane said about a thunderstorm? No – wait! It was a brainstorm. What I needed to do was write down any ideas as fast as I could without rubbing out or stopping.

'Og, I'm going to have a brainstorm, but don't worry. I don't think there'll be lightning or thunder,' I squeaked to my neighbour. 'At least I hope not.'

I took a deep breath and started writing.

If I could fly, I would fly like a:

- Bird
- Kite
- Rocket
- Aeroplane
- Hawk (Eeek – no!!)
- Bumblebee (NO-NO-NO!)
- Squirrel
- Dragon

- Balloon
- Shooting Star
- Hamster

'Brainstorm is over,' I called to Og. 'I'm still fine.'

'BOING-BOING!' Og said, splashing in the water side of his tank.

It was a pretty good list. It would be nice to fly like a kite, drifting along with the breeze . . . unless I got caught in a tree branch. That would be unsqueakably bad!

I like shooting stars, but it might be a little bit *too* exciting for a small creature like me!

I know there are flying squirrels. Squirrels are rodents like me. If some squirrels could fly, why not hamsters?

I'm pretty sure I'd be the very first. I'd probably become famous for flying. Maybe I'd even be on TV!

I picked up my pencil and started to write. At last I had an idea and I wrote it down right away.

Hurray! The page wasn't blank any more!

I glanced up at the clock.

I'd been so busy writing, I'd forgotten that Aldo had said Gigi was lonely.

Luckily, there was still time left before the morning sun peeked through the window.

I jiggled the lock on my cage and, as usual, the door swung open. I'm glad none of my human friends have discovered that it doesn't really lock.

'Og, I'm going to visit Gigi,' I said. 'After all, she doesn't have a friend like you.'

He hopped up and down. 'BOING!'

I could tell he thought it was a good idea.

I grabbed on to the table leg and slid down to the floor, then scrambled across the floor to the door.

'I'll be back soon!' I squeaked as I hunkered down and crawled under the door.

Room 12 is down the hall from Room 26, and Gigi's cage was on a table by the window, just like mine.

I scurried towards the table and looked up. The room was dark, but I could see a large furry brown shape in the cage.

I raised my nose and sniffed. Yep, that was a guinea pig, all right!

'Hi, Gigi,' I squeaked. 'It's me – Humphrey.'

The furry shape didn't move.

I went closer to the table.

'Gigi? It's Humphrey. Remember me – the hamster from Room 26?' I asked.

Not a sound. Not a wiggle.

I was getting worried.

Was Gigi cross with me? Was Gigi ill? Was Gigi . . . something even *worse* than being ill?

'GIGI!' I squeaked at the top of my lungs. 'ARE YOU OKAY?'

Still, she didn't budge.

I looked around. The cord from the blinds was hanging down near the floor, just like in Room 26.

I rushed over, grabbed the cord and began swinging. The harder I swung, the higher I went until I was level with the top of the table.

Then, when the timing seemed right, I let go of the cord and leaped on to the table.

I did two somersaults and ended up near to the cage.

Gigi didn't move.

I moved closer to the cage and stared at the mound of brown fur.

If Gigi was breathing, I sure couldn't tell.

I took a deep breath and shouted. 'GIGI! ARE YOU ALL RIGHT?'

Suddenly, Gigi leaped up and gave a very unhamster-like squeal.

'WHEEEEEE!'

It startled me so much, I did a backward somersault away from the cage and let out an enormous 'SQUEEEEEEEAK!'

'WHEEEEEEE!' she squealed again.

My heart was pounding, but I managed to take a deep breath and say, 'Gigi, it's just me. Humphrey, from Room 26.'

After all, we had met once before.

'Humphrey?' she whispered. 'You scared me. I thought you were a monster!'

'And I thought you were ill. Or worse!' I squeaked back.

Gigi yawned. 'I was sleeping.'

She sure is a sound sleeper!

'Why aren't *you* sleeping?' she asked. 'It's night-time.'

'Because I'm not sleepy at night,' I told her.

'Well, guinea pigs sleep at night, like humans,' she explained.

'Oh.' I was disappointed. After all, I had lots of free time at night.

'It gets awfully lonely here after school.' Gigi shivered. 'At the pet shop, there were so many animals, I was never alone.'

'Pet shop?' I asked. 'What pet shop?'

'Pet-O-Rama,' Gigi replied.

That word made my whiskers wiggle. 'Pet-O-Rama?' I squeaked. 'I came from Pet-O-Rama, too! Say, does Carl still work there?'

'He sure does,' Gigi said. 'I kind of miss him.'

'Being a classroom pet is a lot more fun than living in a pet shop,' I said. 'You'll see.'

The room was getting light. It was time for me to leave.

'Next time, I won't come so late,' I told Gigi.

'Thanks,' she said. 'Please come back again.'

'I will!' I said as I scurried away.

As I slid under the door, I heard Gigi say, 'I'm sorry I thought you were a monster!'

'I'm sorry I scared you!' I squeaked.

Once I was back in Room 26, I raced for the cord of the blinds and swung up again.

'She thought I was a monster,' I told Og as I slid past his cage. 'Imagine that!'

But by the time my friends started streaming into Room 26, I was sound asleep.

Because hamsters *often* enjoy sleeping during the day.

My Writer's Ramblings

I finally got an idea!
I really hoped I would.
But I still have a question:
Is it any good?

Ideas Fly

I was wide awake again by the time Mrs Brisbane started to read the dragon book. The author, Cameron Cole, had invented the most clever dragon world. It was close to the human world, but we kept hearing about details that were lots more dragon-ish!

Think of this: they didn't need a grill to have a barbecue. Their tissues were made out of tin foil so they wouldn't catch fire when they sneezed. And since they could make it rain, they had a special group of fire-fighting dragons to put out accidental blazes.

Gil enjoyed his tour of their cloud. But one thing bothered him a lot: how could a young knight like him help his new dragon friends?

Everybody groaned when she closed the book.

Helpful-Holly raised her hand. 'Mrs Brisbane, how do you think Cameron Cole got all those wonderful ideas?'

'He must have used his imagination a lot,' Mrs Brisbane said. 'How do *you* think the author came up with those ideas, class?'

'He had a gigantic brainstorm – like a hurricane!' Simon said. 'Or a brain-icane!'

My friends giggled.

'Maybe he saw a real dragon,' Cassie said. I could tell she still wasn't sure whether dragons were real or not.

'Maybe he saw a bearded dragon like Pearl,' Nicole said.

'Maybe he dreamed he had birds' wings,' Rolling-Rosie said. 'Like I do.'

'Perhaps he did.' Mrs Brisbane glanced at the clock. 'I think this is a good time to get out your writers' notebooks, class.'

I was unsqueakably curious to find out what my friends had written.

'Mrs Brisbane, is it okay if I changed my mind?' Thomas said. 'I was going to fly to Egypt to see the Pyramids. But then I had a better idea!'

I wished I had as many ideas as Thomas did.

'We're not that far along,' Mrs Brisbane said. 'I suppose so. Would you share what you wrote with us?'

Thomas read from his notebook. 'If I could fly like an eagle, I could go to any football game I wanted to see. I'd swoop over the stadium, following every play. I could watch one game and fly straight to another game and see it, too.'

Somebody said, 'Cool!' I think it was Simon.

I have never been to a football game, but I have seen them on TV at my friends' houses.

It's such a confusing game! Maybe if I had wings, I could hover over the field and figure it out.

'What if it rains?' Tall-Paul asked.

Thomas thought for a second. Then he grinned. 'I'd have waterproof feathers.'

'Thank you, Thomas,' Mrs Brisbane said. 'Why don't you add the part about the waterproof feathers?'

'Yes, miss,' Thomas answered.

I climbed up to the tippy-top of my cage so I could see all my classmates as they read their paragraphs. It was FUN-FUN-FUN to hear about Rosie flying to the Pyramids and seeing that big scary statue called the Sphinx!

I was HAPPY-HAPPY-HAPPY to hear about all the places Kelsey would go to watch the ballet.

And my heart did a little flip-flop when Holly read about how easy it would be to visit her friend Phoebe.

Mrs Brisbane called on Joey.

'Mine's kind of short,' he said.

She told him to go ahead and read it.

'If I could fly, I'd go to Africa so I could see animals in the wild.' Joey looked up. 'That's it.'

'It's a good beginning,' Mrs Brisbane said. 'Next, why don't you name some of the animals you'd most love to see and why you like them?'

Joey looked relieved. 'Okay.'

My whiskers were wiggling when Mrs Brisbane called on Do-It-Now-Daniel. For one thing, he doesn't always get his homework done on time. And for another thing, I'm not sure our teacher liked it when he said he wanted to fly back home and go to bed.

So I was HAPPY-HAPPY-HAPPY to learn

that he *had* done his homework and he'd changed his topic.

'If I could fly like a helicopter, I'd go see my favourite author,' Daniel read. 'His name is D. D. Denby and his books about a magic backpack are really great. I hope he keeps writing them, because I would never get tired of reading more.'

'That's a good start, Daniel,' Mrs Brisbane said. 'I'll bet you said you wanted to fly home and go back to bed because you wanted to finish a magic backpack book.'

Daniel grinned and nodded.

'Tomorrow, I want you to add a descriptive word in front of your noun,' Mrs Brisbane said. 'If you said "bird", put in a word that describes a bird. Can anyone think of one?'

A few hands went up.

'Graceful bird,' Rosie said.

Felipe said, 'Huge bird?'

Cassie said, 'Beautiful bird.'

'Mean bird,' was Simon's suggestion.

Mrs Brisbane said they were all good. I liked them too, except for the mean bird.

'Use your imaginations and be as descriptive

as you can,' she added.

Mrs Brisbane moved on to science and something called gravity. I didn't understand it all, but if we didn't have it, we'd all be floating in space. I guess that would be a little bit like flying.

I decided to take a spin on my hamster wheel. I was HAPPY-HAPPY-HAPPY that gravity kept me from floating away.

After lunch, Sophie came into the room first and headed straight for my cage.

'Humphrey, did you hear me reading about going to the Island of the Parrots and talking with them? Have you ever met a parrot? Do you like parrots? Oh . . . I wish you could talk about them with me!'

'Me too!' I squeaked, but I knew she didn't understand me.

I have to admit, I sometimes have a hard time keeping up with Sophie, because she talks so much and she talks so fast!

•ö•

There's not a lot of time between the end of the school day and when Aldo comes to clean, but I really wanted to see Gigi before she went to sleep, so I took a chance.

When the school was empty, I jiggled my lock-that-doesn't-lock and it swung open as usual.

'Og, I'm going to visit Gigi,' I said. 'But I promise I'll be back before Aldo comes in to clean.'

'BOING!' Og hopped up and down.

I know he worries about me when I'm out of the cage.

I'm *glad* he worries about me. To squeak the truth, I worry about him, too.

I scrunched under the door and hurried as fast as I could to Room 12.

'Hi, Gigi,' I said as I pushed under the door. 'Are you awake?'

'Oh, yes, Humphrey,' Gigi said in her soft voice. 'I don't think I'll sleep at all tonight.'

'Why not?' I asked. 'Wait, I'm coming up there.'

I grabbed on to the blinds' cord, swung my way up to the table and made the big leap.

I slid right past Gigi's cage!

'Whoa! Sorry,' I said as I scrambled back. 'Don't worry – it happens sometimes. Now what's this about not sleeping?'

Gigi shivered. 'I'm scared, Humphrey.'

'What are you scared of?' I asked.

Gigi moved closer to where I was standing. 'Ms Mac said I have to go home with one of the students this weekend.' She stopped shivering and started shaking.

'That will be fun!' I squeaked. 'I love going home with my classmates.'

Really, that's the best part about being a classroom pet.

'It sounds scary to me,' Gigi said. 'Humans are so large and so loud and so *different*. And what am I supposed to *do*?'

'Don't worry about a thing,' I told her. 'The humans are nice and they'll love you. Of course, if you entertain them a little with squeaks and tricks, it makes them happy.'

'Oh.' Gigi sighed. 'I don't know any tricks.'

'That's all right,' I assured her. 'They'll think anything you do is a trick. Listen, don't be frightened. I've been to many human homes and I've always had a GREAT-GREAT-GREAT time.'

Gigi shivered again.

'If you feel scared, remember that your friend Humphrey says everything will be all right!' I tried to sound encouraging.

Suddenly I noticed the time.

'Uh-oh! I have to get back to my cage before Aldo comes in to clean,' I said as I slid down the table leg. 'Remember what I said!'

'Thanks, Humphrey. I'll try!' Gigi squeaked back.

After Aldo had cleaned the room, Og and I were alone again.

'Gigi's worried about going home with a student,' I told him.

'BOING-BOING-BOING!' he twanged.

I was sorry I'd said it, because Og doesn't get to go home with classmates at the weekend the way I do. (Frogs can go without food longer than hamsters.)

But Og has gone with me to Mrs Brisbane's house, which is something we both LOVE-LOVE-LOVE.

'I think she'll be all right,' I told Og.

He didn't answer.

I opened my notebook and read what I'd written the night before.

'If I could, I would fly like a flying squirrel all over the world,' I read.

'BOING!' Og said.

Eeek! I hadn't realized I was reading out loud.

'Do you like it?' I asked.

All I heard was Og splashing around in his tank.

'I don't think I like it either,' I muttered.

Was it as interesting as Daniel's helicopter trip to see his favourite author?

Or Rosie, flying like a bird to see the Sphinx?

Or Simon, breathing fire on a pizza in Italy?

Did my big brainstorm turn out to be drizzle?

I sighed and read it again.

And after a while, I picked up my pencil and added one word. I put 'speedy' in front of 'flying squirrel'.

My Writer's Ramblings

I liked my idea last night.
I liked it quite a bit.
But when I read it back tonight,
I'm not so sure of it!

Bear? Where?

The next day, as Mrs Brisbane read about the war of the dragons – yes, they now were at war – I thought about what a great imagination Cameron Cole had.

And when my friends shared their paragraphs, which were getting longer, I thought about what great imaginations *they* had.

Small-Paul had such a big imagination that he changed his space shuttle into a time-travel machine that would take him into the future. 'It's possible, you know,' he said.

'Einstein said that. He was a great scientist with a huge brain,' Thomas said. 'And lots of hair!'

Einstein may have had a huge brain, but

Small-Paul was a very smart human with a huge imagination. Imagine – travelling to the future!

'Did you hear that,' I squeaked to Og. 'Instead of being here today, we'd be here next week!'

'If I could travel to the future, the maths test would already be over,' Daniel said.

Everyone laughed about that.

'I think you'd better study anyway,' Mrs Brisbane said. 'In case time travel doesn't work.'

While my friends dreamed of flying to Italy, football games and even the future, I was stuck with a silly idea about a flying squirrel.

I was so busy worrying about my imagination, I didn't even remember that it was Friday and that I'd be going home with one of my classmates.

Near the end of the day, Mrs Brisbane reminded me.

'Felipe?' she said. 'Are you all set to take Humphrey home?'

'Yes!' Felipe answered with a big smile.

When the bell rang, he hurried over to the table.

'My dad will be here any minute,' he said. 'He's home today because he's working tonight.'

'Just like Aldo!' I squeaked.

I was looking forward to meeting Mr Garcia. It turned out that he was actually Dr Garcia! He soon arrived and helped carry my cage and food out to the car. Felipe's little brother was there, too. His name was Carlos.

'Bye, Og! Have a good weekend!' I shouted to my friend as we left Room 26.

I don't know if he could hear me because Mrs Brisbane had put a cloth over my cage. It was chilly outside.

It was nice and warm in Felipe's house, though.

Felipe put my cage in the room he shared with Carlos.

They had interesting beds that were stacked on top of each other. There was a little ladder so that someone could get to the bed on top. It reminded me of the little ladder in my cage!

'I have the top bunk,' Felipe said.

'When I'm bigger, *I* get the top bunk,' Carlos said.

'Now, remember,' Felipe told his brother. 'I'm supposed to take care of Humphrey. So don't open his cage or touch him or put anything in his cage, okay? Hamsters need to be treated well.'

'Thanks!' I squeaked and Carlos giggled.

'Can I look at him?' Carlos asked.

Felipe nodded.

'Can I talk to him?'

'Yes, you can talk to him, but that's all,' Felipe said.

'Okay,' Carlos replied.

Carlos looked a little disappointed, so I climbed up my little ladder to the top of my tree branch.

'Look!' Carlos said.

Then I leaped from my tree branch to the side of the cage.

Carlos jumped up and down and squealed.

When I scurried down the side of my cage and dropped to the floor, Carlos jumped up and down and giggled. He sure liked to jump.

Since he was enjoying the show, I hopped on my wheel and began to spin.

Carlos jumped up and down and clapped.

'Don't do anything to scare him,' Felipe said.

But I wasn't scared at all!

Later, Felipe's mum came home and his dad went to work at the hospital.

Felipe and Carlos went to talk to their mum and left me alone in his room.

After a while, Carlos came back to see me.

'Hi, Humphy,' he said.

He didn't say my name correctly, but I didn't mind. After all, he was pretty young.

'Here's my friend, Bear,' he continued. 'Bear, say "hi" to Humphy.'

I know that a bear is a huge, furry wild animal with large teeth. But I didn't see a bear in the room. In fact, I didn't see anyone except for Carlos.

Carlos looked up.

'What's that?' he asked.

Then he paused. 'Oh, he's a hamster,' he said to the air. 'That's kind of like a mouse.'

I don't think a hamster is very much like a mouse, but I didn't argue.

Carlos paused as if he were listening to someone. But I didn't see anyone or hear anything.

Carlos nodded. 'Bear says you're really cute,' he told me. 'He wishes he had a hamster like you.'

I scrambled up to the tippy-top of my cage and looked down, in case Bear was lying on the floor.

I still didn't see anyone but Carlos.

Did I need glasses? Do they even make glasses for hamsters?

Carlos looked up and chuckled. 'That's funny! Humphy, Bear made a joke. He said you're *furry cute*. Get it? Like *very* cute. *Furry* cute!'

It was funny, but I didn't laugh, because I was trying to figure out where Bear *was*.

'Bear makes a lot of jokes,' Carlos said.

'Great!' I squeaked. 'But where is he?'

Carlos giggled. 'Did you hear him, Bear? He's talking.'

And so it went.

Bear told jokes and Carlos laughed.

Then Carlos whispered something to Bear and burst out laughing.

It would have been a lot of fun except for one thing: there was no Bear . . . not anywhere I could see!

Then I had an idea. Maybe Bear was invisible, like a ghost. I don't even want to *think* about ghosts!

I raced into my sleeping hut.

·ö·

Later, Mrs Garcia put Carlos to bed first.

'Goodnight, Mama,' Carlos said. 'Will you say goodnight to Bear, too?'

His mother smiled. 'Where is he?'

Good question!

'He's right here, next to me,' Carlos said. 'He likes it better here than his cave.'

He tugged at the blanket. 'Don't hog the covers, Bear,' he said.

Mrs Garcia smiled. 'Goodnight, Bear.'

She turned down the lights and left the room. I stayed in my sleeping hut and kept my eyes on Carlos's bed, in case Bear was a ghost.

A little later, Felipe climbed the ladder to the top bunk.

I'm usually asleep for part of the night, but that night I kept my eyes wide open all night long.

Things were quiet for several hours and then I saw it: a pale white form floating around the room . . . just like a ghost. And it was as big as a bear. In fact, maybe it *was* a bear!

First, it bent over Carlos's bed and hovered over it.

Then it reached up to Felipe's bed and hovered over *it*.

I crossed my toes and hoped that it wouldn't hover over my cage!

I remembered how I'd told Gigi there was nothing to worry about when visiting humans' homes. I didn't tell her there might be ghosts!

Then the white bear shape whispered, 'Sleep well, my boys.'

The ghost floated out of the room and didn't come back again.

But I kept my eyes on the door all night long.

I must have dozed off at some point, because the next thing I knew, the sun was streaming through the windows, and when I poked my head out of my sleeping hut, the boys' beds were empty.

'Eeek!' I squeaked, thinking the bear ghost had taken them away.

But right after that, Felipe and Carlos came back into their room, fully dressed.

And they were arguing.

'Just 'cause you can't see Bear doesn't mean he's not real,' Carlos said.

Felipe was annoyed. 'He's *imaginary*. He's your *imaginary* friend. He's not *real*.'

'Yes, he is!' Carlos argued.

'Yes, he is!' I squeaked. 'I think I saw him last night.'

Mrs Garcia came into the room. She was wearing a long white dressing gown. 'Boys, let's not argue, all right?' she said. 'You'll upset Humphrey.'

She came up close to my cage and looked down at me. 'Humphrey, I hope I didn't scare you when I came in last night to make sure the boys were warm enough. I must have looked strange with my bathrobe and my shower cap!'

'You looked like a big white bear!' I squeaked, but I know she didn't understand me.

She turned towards her sons. 'Why don't you settle down, you two? Felipe, I think you probably have some homework to do.'

Felipe nodded.

Mrs Garcia led Carlos out of the room and Felipe flopped down on his bed.

'That imaginary friend drives me *loco*,' he said. 'Crazy. Does he really believe Bear is real?'

I thought for a moment. *I* believed he was real.

'I need to work on my paragraph,' Felipe said. 'I'll read you what I have so far.'

He picked up his notebook from his desk and opened it.

'If I could fly, I'd fly like a glowing lightning bolt and go straight to the theme park, all by myself. I'd ride the Thunderbolt roller-coaster over and over again,' he read. 'Then I'd ride the Raging Rockets and the swinging pirate ship. I'd move into the fun house and live there for ever – and I'd never have to queue.'

Felipe let out a huge sigh. 'Mrs Brisbane wasn't sure whether lightning actually flew, but she said she liked it. I'm not sure it's as good as it could be.'

'It's GREAT-GREAT-GREAT,' I said. 'A lot better than mine.'

I suddenly felt terrible, because I hadn't even

written a whole paragraph.

'Don't listen to Carlos and his talk about the imaginary friend,' he said. 'Mum and Dad say he'll grow out of it. They say lots of kids have imaginary friends.'

I moved closer to Felipe. 'They do?'

'Don't pay any attention to him,' Felipe added.

It was hard not to pay attention to Carlos. For one thing, he was nice. And his imaginary friend was interesting, even if he was a little scary.

For the rest of the day, Felipe and I had fun.

He made a maze with blocks and let me roll through it in my hamster ball.

I didn't even mind when Carlos said, 'Look, Bear! Look at Humphy go!'

There was no Bear, except in our imaginations.

And later that night, when the boys were tucked in bed, I realized that I had an imagination after all.

Otherwise, I would have never seen Bear!

My Writer's Ramblings

I have to say this weekend,
I had a great big scare.
But I was scared of something
That wasn't even there!

Beginner's Brainstorm

'Did you have a nice weekend?' I asked Og when my cage was back on the table on Monday morning.

'BOING-BOING!' he said. He sounded cheerful, but I'm sure he missed me.

We started the day with English. We were studying words that sound exactly the same, but can have different meanings when they are spelled differently. Mrs Brisbane wrote the word for them on the board: *Homophones*. I hope that word is never in a spelling test!

These are words such as *blew* and *blue*, or *ate* and *eight*.

Mrs Brisbane also wrote funny sentences on the board.

The monkey ate eight bananas.
The boat shop had a sail sale.

These words can be pretty funny if you get them mixed up.

For instance, if you heard someone say, 'Don't touch the *hair* on my head' you might think they were saying, 'Don't touch the *hare* on my head.'

But it would only make sense if the person happened to have a rabbit on top of his head!

Humans have a pretty funny language and it's a lot more complicated than 'SQUEAK-SQUEAK-SQUEAK!'

Mrs Brisbane said there was a test coming up, so I made sure to write down all the words. *Two, too. Grown, groan. Reed, read.*

Hurry-Up-Harry raised his hand. 'I have one for you,' he said. 'My dog told the *flea* to *flee.*'

Mrs Brisbane liked that one. I did too. Harry has a good imagination!

She also gave us an assignment to come up with a sentence using homophones of our own.

Then we moved on to science.

I already knew about gravity, but now Mrs Brisbane talked about *force* and *mass*. I was unsqueakably confused when she talked about pushing and pulling and weight.

(*Wait* and *weight* would be good words for our test.)

After lunch came the part of the day I'd been waiting for. Mrs Brisbane asked my friends to open their writing journals.

I couldn't wait to hear how my friends had used their imaginations to make their writing even better.

'If I could fly like a speeding jet, I'd go to Winfield to see my friend Phoebe every day because I miss her so much,' Holly read. 'We'd do all our favourite things. We'd pretend to be rock stars and sing along to our favourite songs. We'd play Monopoly and make smoothies. And we'd make friendship bracelets because we're best friends. My parents said I can go and visit Phoebe during the Easter holidays but I wish I didn't have to wait.'

I wished she didn't have to wait, either.

I loved Thomas's story about going to three football games in one day and Simon's description of all kinds of yummy Italian food.

Cassie wrote, 'If I could fly like a soaring seagull, I'd fly to the seaside and sit on the beach. The only sounds I'd hear would be the crashing waves and the cries of the other seagulls. It would be a peaceful place.'

I think even Calm-Down-Cassie, who is very excitable, would be calm there. But I think I'd have trouble relaxing with those seagulls around me with their sharp beaks.

'Thank you, Cassie,' Mrs Brisbane said. 'It's important to write about something you'd really like to do. That's why your paragraph is coming along so well. And don't forget to keep adding more details.'

Joey, on the other paw, still seemed to be having as much trouble with his paragraph as I was. Mrs Brisbane was encouraging and Joey said he'd try again.

Why did everyone in class have a good imagination . . . except Joey and me?

Then Mrs Brisbane read from the dragon book again.

When Gil Goodfriend asked why he was chosen to

help, Goldie said, *'Because of your invention.'*

Gil was puzzled.

Goldie continued. 'We have a very good view of Bumpshire from our cloud. We saw the amazing machine you built to turn snow into ice cream. We have never seen something so clever! Anyone who can figure that out is the person to help us.'

He explained that the dragons had discovered an ancient book that held the secrets of how the last dragon war had been won. But there was a big problem. The instructions were hidden in codes and riddles that the dragons couldn't figure out.

'Are you listening, Og?' I squeaked to my neighbour. 'Codes and riddles!'

Og didn't make a sound. I think he was waiting to hear what happened next.

Mrs Brisbane turned the page and continued.

'If you can solve the riddles and work out the codes, we can use special swords and shields to make magic that only works in the sky,' Goldie said. 'You are our only hope.'

Mrs Brisbane's eyes grew wide as she read the next part.

Gil's hands trembled as he opened the book.

I think my paws were trembling, too.

Gil worked for days to figure out most of the codes and many of the riddles.

But the most important discovery he made was this: The secret to controlling the dragons was to speak backwards. (So the last part of that sentence would read: Sdrawkcab kaeps ot saw snogard eht gnillortnoc ot terces eht. It was funny hearing Mrs Brisbane try to read *that*.)

From then on, when he commanded the bad dragons to stop the lightning or hail or whatever horrible weather they were creating, he said it backwards. That – combined with the magic shield – made everything the evil dragons did reverse direction and strike their own cloud. By the time Gil left, the bad dragons' village was frozen solid!

Cameron Cole, the author, must have a brain overflowing with imagination! Castles, codes, shields and secrets! But the sad thing was, we were almost at the very end of the book.

Sophie stayed after school to ask Mrs Brisbane a question. 'I have some more ideas about the island with the parrots.' I could hear the excitement in her voice. 'Is it all right if I write more than a paragraph?'

'Of course. But make sure everything you write fits in and is important,' Mrs Brisbane replied.

'I will!' Sophie said. 'Because I had this dream about parrots, I told you.'

'Yes,' Mrs Brisbane said as she turned towards the door. Sophie turned, too.

'I've never had a parrot because, well, my parents said I'd have to wait,' Sophie continued.

'Uh-huh,' our teacher said, walking towards the door. Sophie walked with her.

'But I'd love to hear them talk,' Sophie said. 'I'd like a dog, but they don't talk.'

Mrs Brisbane nodded and opened the door. 'Put it in your paragraph,' she said. 'And have a nice evening.'

Sometimes, even I'm surprised by our teacher. She'd managed to be a good listener

and also make sure Sophie didn't miss her bus
. . . all at the same time!

·ö·

Once the car park was empty, I jiggled the lock-that-doesn't-lock and slipped under the door.

I couldn't wait to hear how Gigi's weekend had gone.

Since it was still early, she was awake.

'Oh, Humphrey, I was hoping you would come,' she said.

I raced towards the table and looked up.

'Did you have a good time?' I asked.

'Yes!' Gigi exclaimed. 'I had the best time ever! The humans were so nice and they talked to me and played with me all weekend. And they were very gentle.'

'I told you so,' I squeaked.

'Now I'll never be worried about going home with a student,' she continued. 'Nothing scary could happen to me.'

Nothing scary? How about an invisible bear? Or maybe even a ghost!

I decided not to tell Gigi about my weekend.

'Now you see how much fun it is to be a classroom pet,' I said.

I glanced up at the big clock on the wall. 'Oops, I've got to get back to Room 26. Aldo will be here any minute.'

'Come and see me again, Humphrey!' Gigi called after me.

I got back to my cage a few minutes before Aldo arrived.

'I got an A in the test!' he shouted when the lights came on. 'The best grade in the class!'

'Congratulations!' I squeaked.

'BOING-BOING-BOING-BOING!' Og said in his twangy voice.

Aldo took a bow. 'Thank you, my friends. And now, time to get to work.'

I always enjoy watching Aldo at work.

He always does things in the same order: dusting, sweeping, emptying the bins.

He never forgets to sweep the corners of the room and underneath every desk.

Sometimes he balances his broom on one finger. That's his favourite trick. But that night, he amazed me by leaning his head back and balancing the broom on his chin.

That's talent!

Aldo always does the best job he possibly can. I try to do the same in my job as a classroom pet.

But I wasn't doing a very good job on my writing.

If Mrs Brisbane had to give me a grade on my paragraph, she wouldn't give me an A.

Or a B. Or even a C.

And that made me feel BAD-BAD-BAD.

When Aldo was gone, I got out my notebook and looked at what I'd written.

If I could fly, I'd fly like a speedy flying squirrel all over the world.

I sighed. It wasn't any good, but even worse, it wasn't really true. And Mrs Brisbane had told us to write about something we'd really like to do.

I would not like to be a squirrel, not even a flying squirrel. I love being a hamster!

At first, I'd thought maybe only humans have imaginations.

But at Felipe's house, I'd imagined I'd seen a

ghost, when all I'd seen was Felipe's nice mother in a white dressing gown! That took a *lot* of imagination.

So if I could imagine bad things, why couldn't I imagine good things?

I stared and stared at the page until I heard a loud rumbling sound.

'BOING-BOING-BOING-BOING!' Og said in a worried tone.

The rumble was followed by a loud crash!

Og hopped around his tank. 'BOING!!!!!'

I was too scared to squeak!

Suddenly, rain began pelting the window next to our table. A bright flash lit up the room, followed by another loud crash.

It was a thunderstorm!

I don't like thunderstorms, but at least I knew what was making all that noise. At first, I thought the rumbling was in my brain!

I jiggled the lock-that-doesn't-lock and headed over to Og's tank. 'Og, it's all right. It's just a thunderstorm. You know what they're like.'

Og stopped hopping and stared at me with his big, bulging eyes.

Who knows what he was thinking, but he finally said, 'BOING!'

I was pretty sure he understood me. 'Gigi might not know how noisy thunderstorms sound in these classrooms when you're all alone. She's probably afraid,' I said. 'Will you be all right if I leave for a few minutes to see how she's doing?'

Og stared at me again, but his head moved a little. It was almost like a nod.

'BOING!' he agreed.

Soon, I was scurrying down the hallway again.

All the rumbling, crashing and flashes of light made my whiskers wiggle, but I didn't turn back.

Once I was in Room 12, I raced towards Gigi's cage. I figured she wasn't sleeping this time!

'Gigi!' I squeaked at the top of my lungs, but there was a huge crash that rattled the windows and I don't think she heard me.

So I grabbed the cord and swung UP-UP-UP and leaped on to the table.

'Gigi, it's all right,' I said. 'It's a thunderstorm.

It's part of nature, like we are!'

My friend was huddling in the corner. I think she was shaking.

'Don't be afraid,' I said, even though the thunder made my small ears throb. 'It won't last long. And it won't hurt you.'

'Are you sure?' she softly squeaked.

'Pretty sure,' I replied. After all, I had to be honest. 'I'll stay here with you until it goes away.'

It wasn't long before the crashes sounded farther away and the flashes of light weren't as bright.

'See?' I said. 'It's moving on.'

The rain continued, but after a few minutes, there was no more thunder and lightning.

'Thanks for staying with me,' Gigi said. 'You're a good friend.'

'Any time, Gigi,' I answered. 'You're a good friend, too. But I'd better see how Og is doing.'

'I hope to meet him someday. Tell him I said hello.'

'I'll do it!' I said as I slid down the table leg and headed back to Room 26.

'Og, are you all right?' I asked when I got

back to our table.

I guess he was, because he was swimming around in the water side of his tank.

'Gigi said to tell you hello,' I told him. 'And she hopes to meet you someday.'

Just then, Og leaped up out of the water and said, 'BOING!'

I guess he wanted to meet Gigi, too. But how could a frog in a tank and a guinea pig with a lock-that-does-lock ever come face to face?

I rested for a while, and after a snack and a nice drink of water, I opened my notebook again.

That thunderstorm had really rattled my brain. In fact, I'd felt like the thunderstorm was *in* my brain, like a brainstorm!

And a brainstorm was just what I needed.

Mrs Brisbane had said to write about things we like to do. She also said to write down any idea that came into our heads without stopping.

So I wrote this down:

Things I Like to Do:

I took a deep breath, and then there was a rumbling in my brain. Under that heading, I wrote:

- Be a classroom pet
- Help my friends with their problems
- Go to my friends' houses
- Go to all kinds of interesting new places
- Help my teacher with her problems
- Have adventures outside my cage
- Meet new friends
- Try new things
- Visit old friends, like Phoebe
- Help everybody with their problems

My paw was getting tired, so I stopped and read what I'd written. It was pretty clear that I liked to have adventures and help my friends. If I could combine those two things, I'd be unsqueakably happy.

'Og, I think I had a brainstorm,' I squeaked. 'Or at least a brainshower.'

'BOING-BOING!' Og sounded cheerful.

'And a brainshower is a start,' I added.

ᵒ̈ᵒ̈   ᵒ̈ᵒ̈

My Writer's Ramblings

At first there was some drizzle,
And then a lot of rain,
And finally I had it:
A big storm in my brain!

Little House in Sophie's Room

'Humphrey, I hope you can come home with me this weekend,' Sophie told me on Tuesday morning. 'Because you've never been to my house and it would be so much fun to have you there and I'd take really good care of you.'

Sophie paused. Once she gets started talking, she hardly ever pauses.

'Of course, there's *Timothy*,' she said.

'Oh,' I squeaked. 'Who is Timothy?' I wondered if Timothy was an imaginary bear.

'But we'll have fun anyway,' she said. 'I promise you! I have so many things to show you – my room, my family, my games, my panda . . .'

Sometimes, I stare at Sophie's mouth because it moves and moves and moves. Really, I don't know how she can talk like that.

I guess Joey doesn't know, either, because he walked by while Sophie was talking.

'What's going on?' he said.

'What do you mean?' Sophie asked.

'Why are you talking so much to Humphrey?' Joey said.

'Because . . .' Sophie replied. 'Because I hope he's coming home with me this weekend. It's my turn!'

Joey scratched his head. 'I wish he could come home with me. I've never had him at my house. Either my mum is too busy or my dad is coming to visit. He lives out of town and I don't see him a lot.'

'I know!' I squeaked.

Just then, Mrs Brisbane asked everyone to sit down. Joey moved on, but Sophie kept talking to me.

'I'll clean your cage and give you treats!' Sophie continued. 'I'll tell you all about the dream I had. And I'll tell you . . .' Sophie stopped talking because Mrs Brisbane came right up to her and told her it was time to sit down.

Sophie looked so downcast, for a second I

wasn't very happy with Mrs Brisbane. I knew she had to start class again, but Sophie lights up when she's talking.

But I have to admit, she talks a TINY-TINY-TINY bit too much.

I wonder why?

I didn't have too much time to think about Sophie, because we talked about our assignment about *homophones* (or *honomyns* or *homynomynyms*). My friends had come up with all kinds of funny combinations.

Harry wrote a sentence about a *pale pail.*

Nicole wrote about a hairless bear: a *bare bear.* (Of course, the thought of Carlos's imaginary Bear still made me shiver.)

Thomas had this sentence: 'The football player was injured and had to *heal* his *heel.*'

Kelsey had almost the same sentence, but hers was about a ballet dancer.

'I *see* the *sea*,' Cassie read.

'*Rows* of *roses rose* from the ground,' Tall-Paul said. How clever to come up with one word with three meanings!

Joey's was simple, but also clever. 'Number *one won* the game.'

I didn't have a chance to read mine out loud, of course. But I had one: 'I had *pain* in my paw when I broke the window *pane*.' I was proud of that!

·ỏ·

During the week, I kept working on my idea in my little notebook.

Even though the weather was calm, I tried to brainstorm about how I'd like to help my friends.

- Help Holly visit Phoebe
- Help Mrs Brisbane visit her son Jason in Japan
- Help Joey see more of his dad
- Help Cassie go to the seaside
- Help Sophie go to the parrot island
- Help Simon go to Italy
- Help Kelsey go to the ballet

As you can see, it was a LONG-LONG-LONG list!

On Friday morning, Sophie handed Mrs Brisbane a piece of paper. 'Here's my permission slip! I was really worried that my parents would say "no", because they're so busy, but I promised them I'd do all the work and there wouldn't be any mess or any noise.'

I was pretty sure what that permission slip was all about. And I vowed that I'd do my part to make sure she kept that promise.

For the rest of the day, Sophie kept glancing over at my cage.

While my friends were working on their vocabulary words and maths problems, she sneaked peeks at me. Once she even waved. (Luckily, Mrs Brisbane didn't notice.)

When the rest of the class – including me – was listening to an amazing chapter from the dragon story, Sophie just stared at me.

Later, while the other students read from their writing journals, Sophie didn't pay a bit of attention. Instead, she was smiling at me.

Mrs Brisbane had to call her name three times when it was her turn to read her work.

I knew our teacher was annoyed, but after she heard Sophie's paragraph about flying like a parrot to join other parrots on an island, she said, 'Excellent work.'

That made me smile, even though the idea of being alone on an island with large and noisy birds is not my idea of fun!

'o'

'Oh, Humphrey, we're going to have so much fun,' Sophie said after school as Mrs Brisbane helped her carry my cage and other important items such as my Nutri-Nibbles and Mighty Mealworms.

'I'm sure we will!' I squeaked.

I only wished I didn't have to leave Og behind.

'BOING-BOING!' he called as I was carried out of Room 26.

'I'll be back soon,' I called back.

Usually a parent or grandparent comes to pick me up. Sometimes I take the bus (which is noisy and bumpy).

But this day, the parent of another student picked us up.

His first name was Carter. His last name was George. So he really had two first names. Or two last names. He wasn't a student in Room 26, but he lived next door to Sophie.

Of course, I couldn't see Carter or his mum, because Mrs Brisbane had put a cloth over my cage to keep me warm. It was COLD-COLD-COLD outside.

'I get to have Humphrey all to myself,' Sophie told her friend.

'Can I see him?' Carter picked up a corner of the cloth and peeked at me. I still couldn't see him. All I could see was a giant eye. It was a friendly giant eye, though.

'I sure wish I had a hamster,' he said. 'Or a classroom hamster. Our room is really boring.'

I can't imagine a classroom *without* a pet! Even a frog like Og would be more fun than not having a pet at all.

When we got to her house, Sophie's mum opened the door and whispered, 'Come on in, but please be quiet.'

Sophie set my cage on a table in the living room and took the cloth off.

'Come and see him, Mum,' she said. 'Isn't he cute?'

'Ssssh,' Mrs Kaminski said softly.

I looked up at Sophie's mum. She was holding a rolled-up blanket.

'Hello,' I squeaked softly.

'Isn't he cute?' Sophie whispered. 'I'm going to clean his cage and feed him and give him fresh water and . . .'

'Sweetie, tell me later,' Mrs Kaminski whispered.

Sophie kneeled next to the low table so her face was at the same level as mine.

'Welcome to my house, Humphrey,' she said. 'I'm so happy you're going to stay here.'

'Me too!' I squeaked.

Sophie stood up. 'Mum, Mrs Brisbane really liked my paragraph. She said it was excellent!'

Suddenly, the blanket made a very loud noise. 'Waaah! Waaah!'

It was so loud, my whiskers wiggled and my ears shook.

Mrs Kaminski sighed. 'Oh, no.' She jiggled the blanket. 'It's all right, baby.'

She made funny clicking sounds with her

tongue and asked Sophie to take me to her room.

'Okay,' Sophie said but she didn't sound happy.

She put my cage on a small table right next to her bed.

'Welcome to my room,' she said. 'Don't worry. Timothy has his own room.'

Even so, I could still hear him wailing.

'All he does is cry,' Sophie said. 'Sometimes I cry, too.'

'I'm SORRY-SORRY-SORRY,' I said.

I'm always sorry when my friends cry.

'All babies do is cry, eat, and make messy nappies,' she said. 'That's it!'

Got it! There was a baby in that rolled-up blanket and the baby was called Timothy.

'I guess he can't help it, Sophie,' I said.

I wished she could understand my squeaks.

I hopped on my wheel and started spinning. That made Sophie giggle.

'You're so funny, Humphrey,' she said.

I was GLAD-GLAD-GLAD to hear her laugh.

'Did you hear Mrs Brisbane say my work was excellent?' she asked.

'I did!' I squeaked. 'I liked it, too. Even though it was about parrots.'

Sophie reached in the cage and gently picked me up. She held me in one hand and stroked me with the other. 'You're so soft, Humphrey,' she said. 'You're the most handsome hamster I've ever seen.'

'Thanks!' I squeaked.

Next, Sophie gave me a tour of her room. She showed me her desk, her books, her wardrobe full of clothes and toys, her dressing table, her beanbag chair and her panda bear, Pickles. Luckily, Pickles was a toy instead of a *real* panda.

Then she put me inside my hamster ball.

It wasn't so easy to roll around her room, because she had carpet on the floor.

She sat down on the carpet and watched me.

'Mum said that soon Timothy will sleep more and cry less and she'll have more time for me,' she said. 'But that's taking a long time. Dad said that when I was Timothy's age, I cried a lot, too, but I don't remember that. I don't remember being a baby at all.'

I kept listening and rolling as Sophie continued to talk.

I rolled into a corner but managed to back out.

Sophie kept talking.

I rolled under the bed. Even though it was dark under there, I was able to see a sock with blue polka dots.

I rolled out from under the bed.

Sophie was still talking.

And then, something wonderful happened: Sophie's mother came into her room and the baby wasn't with her.

'Hi, Mum!' Sophie said. 'Look, Humphrey's in his hamster ball!'

'Oh, that's so cute,' Mrs Kaminski said.

'He's the smartest hamster in the world,' Sophie said. 'He does all these tricks. Sometimes he hangs from the top of his cage by one hand – I mean paw. And he climbs that ladder and spins on his wheel!'

I rolled close to Mrs Kaminski's foot.

She bent down to look at me. 'Hi, Humphrey,' she said.

I spun the ball in a circle.

Mrs Kaminski yawned. 'Sorry, Humphrey. Timothy kept us awake all night.'

'That was rude,' I squeaked.

'Tomorrow, I'll show you and Dad how to clean his cage,' Sophie said. 'I'm really good at it.'

'Great,' Mrs Kaminski said, yawning again. 'Your dad's plane is about to land, but he has to work on a report tonight. He's working on a big deal.'

'Everything is a big deal,' Sophie muttered.

'What did you say?' her mum asked.

'Nothing.'

Just then, Timothy started wailing again. 'Waaah! Waaah! Waaah!'

Even inside my hamster ball, he sounded LOUD-LOUD-LOUD.

'Oh,' Sophie's mum said. 'I was hoping he'd sleep for a while.'

'Me too,' Sophie said softly.

Her mother hurried out of the room and Sophie picked up my hamster ball.

'Timothy is my brother and I love him,' she said. 'But I don't always *like* him.'

'Maybe you'll like him when he's older,' I squeaked.

'I wish Dad didn't have to work so much,'

she said. 'I wish Timothy didn't cry so much. I wish Mum wasn't tired all the time.'

Sophie took me out of my hamster ball and held me in her hand.

I wiggled my whiskers and twitched my tail, which made her laugh.

'I wish you were my hamster,' she said, which was sooooo sweet of her.

Sophie's mum returned. 'I got him back to sleep. How about a snack?'

'Yes!' Sophie quickly put me back in my cage and followed her mother out of the room.

I crossed my paws and wished that Timothy would have a LONG-LONG-LONG nap.

My wish did not come true.

After a few minutes, I heard it again. 'WAAAH!'

He cried for a while and then Sophie came back in her room, carrying a handful of apple slices.

'Mum and I were having a nice talk,' she said. 'Then *he* started crying again.'

She sat on the bed and broke off a small piece of apple.

'Here, Humphrey.' She opened the door to

my cage. 'I'm not very hungry. You like apples, don't you?'

'Yes!' I squeaked. I happily took the piece of apple. I wasn't very hungry, either, but at least I had my cheek pouch to store it in.

'Let's play,' Sophie said after a while. She went back to her wardrobe and searched through her toys.

'Oh, I forgot about this!' She reached way back in her wardrobe and pulled out something large. 'My doll's house. I haven't played with it for a long time.'

She pushed the doll's house to the middle of the room and carried me over to it.

'See, Humphrey? It's a little house,' she said.

It wasn't like any house I'd ever seen because one side was completely open. There was no wall, so you could see the rooms inside. There was furniture in every room like in a real house, but the pieces were tiny

'It's just your size,' Sophie said.

She set me down in the living room and I began to look around.

I looked at the fireplace and the painting of a vase of flowers. There was also a chair, a blue rug, two lamps and a tiny television.

But what grabbed my attention was the red sofa. It looked so cosy, I had to try it out.

Sophie laughed out loud and raced to the door.

'Mum, come and look at Humphrey in the doll's house!' she shouted.

'I'm feeding Timothy,' her mother called back. 'I'll be there soon.'

Sophie ran back to the doll's house.

I left the sofa and went through a little door to the kitchen with a refrigerator, stove, sink, table and chairs.

While Sophie giggled, I sniffed all around but I'm sorry to say, I didn't see any food in that kitchen!

I went into the dining room – no food there either. So I scrambled up the staircase in the hallway.

The upstairs bedroom had a soft bed that was exactly my size! Of course, I had to try it.

'Mum! Now Humphrey's in bed!' Sophie yelled through the doorway. 'Hurry!'

'In a minute,' Mrs Kaminski called back.

I looked out the window and was about to

climb through when Sophie caught me.

'No, no, Humphrey,' she said. 'You'll hurt yourself if you jump out the window. Here, try the bathroom.'

When I visit my human friends' houses, I almost never go in the bathrooms. Hamsters don't like to get wet.

This one had a tiny sink, a toilet and a little rug.

There was also a hamster-sized bath. It was nice and dry, so I crawled inside.

Sophie giggled. 'Humphrey, you're so funny. Oh! I have an idea.'

She disappeared so I left the bathroom and climbed up another staircase to the attic. There wasn't much there. Some boxes and a trunk.

I checked the little window up there, but it was too small for me to climb through.

By then, Sophie was back. 'Humphrey! Dinner is served in the kitchen.'

I scurried down the stairs, back to the kitchen.

There was food on the table.

'Have some fried chicken and mashed potatoes,' she said. 'With corn on the cob.'

I don't know much about those human foods, so I carefully approached the table and sniffed.

There was no fried chicken, mashed potatoes or corn-on-the-cob there. But there were raisins! I LOVE-LOVE-LOVE raisins.

I quickly gobbled them up. Yum!

'And for dessert, apple pie,' Sophie said, placing another raisin on the table.

I took the raisin and placed it in my cheek pouch for later.

Now I understood. Sophie was using her imagination and pretending the raisins were other food.

'Do you think I'm a good cook?' Sophie asked, laughing.

'The best!' I told her.

I was just about to head upstairs again because there was one room I hadn't visited. But Sophie reached in and picked me up (gently, I'm happy to say) and took me back to my cage.

'I'll be back soon, Humphrey,' she said.

I looked around my cage. It's my house, but it doesn't look anything like a human house. I store my food in my cheek pouch instead of a refrigerator. I never eat fried chicken and mashed potatoes. I use my poo corner instead of a toilet.

It's an unsqueakably nice cage, really.

But somehow, I couldn't stop looking at that little doll's house.

And I couldn't stop thinking about the room I'd missed.

My Writer's Ramblings

My cage is such a cosy place –
I really do approve.
But since I saw the little house
I think I want to move!

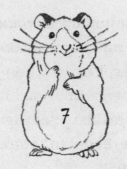

House Hunting

I ate the piece of apple that was stored in my cheek while I stared at the house in the middle of the room.

After a while, Sophie returned with her father.

'See, Dad,' she said, running to my cage. 'It's Humphrey! Isn't he cute?'

Mr Kaminski followed her and bent down to look in my cage.

'Where is he?' he asked.

I poked my head out of my sleeping hut.

Mr Kaminski chuckled. 'Oh, there he is. Hi, Humphrey.'

'HI-HI-HI to you!' I said.

Sophie showed him my water bottle, my

wheel, my ladder and my sleeping hut.

I hopped on my wheel to show her father how fast I could spin.

I could tell he was enjoying himself until his phone rang and he had to answer it.

After he'd left the room, Sophie was VERY-VERY-VERY quiet.

'Business,' she muttered.

I'm not sure exactly what business it was, but it didn't sound like a good thing.

A few minutes later, Mr Kaminski appeared in the doorway. He was still talking on the phone, but he motioned for Sophie to come with him and then moved his hand to his mouth as if he were eating.

'Dinnertime, Humphrey!' she said.

Sophie nicely checked to see that there was food in my dish and then hurried out of the room.

She wasn't gone for long.

'So . . . Timothy is ill and Mum says he has a temperature and Dad's gone out to get him medicine,' Sophie said. 'I watched TV, but you know what? I missed you, Humphrey, because you are my best friend.'

'That's great!' I squeaked.

'*You* always listen to me,' she continued. '*You're* never too busy. *You* don't have to go to work or write reports or take care of babies.'

It was all true, except the part about writing. I write my homework in my notebook, even though no one in Room 26 sees it.

'So maybe you'd like to hear my paragraph,' she said.

'Of course,' I said.

'If I could be a pretty parrot, I'd fly across the ocean to the magical Island of the Parrots,' she read. 'I could tell my parrot pals about my day at school and my friends in Room 26 – and they'd listen! Then they would tell me what it was like to live high in the treetops and be able to fly – and about their parrot classes. And I would listen. That would make me happy because sometimes, people don't listen to me.'

She stopped reading and turned to me. 'What do you think, Humphrey?'

'I think you have a wonderful imagination,' I squeaked.

She giggled at my squeaks.

But now I knew how much it bothered

Sophie that her parents were too busy to listen.

She talked a lot that evening and I listened.

Later, when she went to bed, her mum – carrying the blanket with Timothy inside – tucked her in with a kiss.

Of course, Timothy went, 'Waaah! Waaah!' and Mrs Kaminski hurried out of the room.

The next morning, things hadn't changed much.

Sophie's father was writing his report. Her mother was taking care of Timothy, who seemed to cry more than he slept.

Sophie sat next to my cage and talked. And talked. And talked.

I was glad to listen, but I have to admit, my small hamster ears were getting tired!

Luckily, Carter George came over to visit.

'Look – there's his wheel that he loves to spin on and he has a sleeping hut, a water bottle, a food dish and a ladder to climb. Plus he can roll around in his hamster ball,' Sophie explained.

Carter nodded.

'I'm sorry your class doesn't have a classroom pet,' she continued without stopping to take a breath. 'You could have a hamster or a guinea pig or a bunny or even a frog like Og. He's so funny. Would you like a classroom pet?'

Carter nodded.

'What pet would you like?'

Carter shrugged.

'Did I ever tell you about my dream where I went to the Island of the Parrots and we could talk to each other? I'm writing about it now,' she said. 'Do you like parrots?'

Carter nodded.

Sophie was finally silent for a moment.

Then she asked, 'Don't you have anything to say?'

'Not really,' Carter said. 'I'm not much of a talker.'

So Sophie took me out of my cage and over to the doll's house.

Carter laughed when I went in the bath and then scurried to the bed.

That little bed was so soft and cosy!

Then Sophie put me back in my cage while she and Carter left to play a game.

I have to admit, I was ready for a nap, so I darted into my sleeping hut.

It was cosy, but I kept looking at the doll's house and that REALLY-REALLY-REALLY soft bed.

I stared at it until I went to sleep.

I must have dozed a long time, because when I woke up, Sophie was going to bed.

'Goodnight, Humphrey,' she said with a yawn.

I'm happy to say that Sophie does *not* talk in her sleep!

The next morning, Sophie's mother came into the room *without* Timothy.

'I'm sorry this hasn't been a great weekend for you,' she said. 'Timothy's cried so much. I think he has a cold. It's very hard for babies when they have a cold.'

'I have colds sometimes,' Sophie said.

'Yes, but babies can't tell you what's wrong, so that's a worry,' her mum said. 'And I can't make chicken soup for him the way I do for you.'

I was HAPPY-HAPPY-HAPPY when Mrs Kaminski gave Sophie a hug.

'Are you having fun with Humphrey?' she asked.

Sophie nodded. 'Yes! I'd like to have a pet of my own.'

Mrs Kaminski nodded. 'I know. But I think it would be better to wait until Timothy's a little older.'

I could tell how disappointed Sophie was, although I'm not sure how much I'd enjoy a visit to her house if she got a large dog or cat!

'Do you have homework?' Mrs Kaminski asked.

Sophie started to tell her about the island with the parrots but she didn't get to finish.

'Waaah! Waaah!' Timothy cried.

Mrs Kaminski jumped up.

'I've got to see what's wrong,' she said. 'Your dad has to finish his report by tomorrow.'

'But it's the weekend,' Sophie complained.

'Dad's boss doesn't believe in weekends,' Mrs Kaminski said. 'Come with me.'

Sophie did leave with her mum, but I think she would have liked to sit and talk some more – without Timothy.

When I see my classmates having a problem, I always try to help them. So I hopped on my wheel and started spinning, thinking about what I could do.

I wanted to tell the Kaminskis that Sophie needed someone to listen to her. I knew she loved the baby, but she felt left out.

My problem was that I couldn't tell them, because even though I understand humans, they don't understand me.

If I said, 'Please help Sophie by spending time listening to her,' all they would hear would be 'SQUEAK-SQUEAK-SQUEAK.'

How could I get their attention?

Then, I thought of a Plan.

It was a risky Plan, because I don't want any humans to discover my lock-that-doesn't-lock. If they did, they'd probably fix it, and where would I be? Stuck in my cage for ever!

Still, Sophie needed my help. And I did want to go back and explore that little house a bit more.

On Sunday afternoon, Sophie worked on her homework. But that didn't keep her from talking.

She wrote for a while and then said, 'Humphrey, do you think there are pink and purple parrots? I've never seen one, but parrots come in all colours. Oh, I wish I could really talk to them!'

Then she wrote some more. 'Humphrey, which do you like better? I first wrote "pretty parrot", and then I wrote "gorgeous parrot", but now I might change it to "stunning parrot" or even "splendid parrot". What do you think?'

'I'm not sure,' I squeaked back. 'I like them all.'

I hoped she didn't think I actually *liked* parrots. But I liked what she wrote about them.

I was surprised when her father came in.

'How's the homework coming along?' he asked.

'I'm finishing,' Sophie said. 'How does "splendid parrot" sound?'

Her father smiled and said, 'It sounds splendid to me. I'm sorry my report is taking so long. Your mum has had a tough time with

Timothy being ill. I can't help her as much as I'd like, so why don't we order a pizza?'

The smile on Sophie's face was splendid!

'See you later, Humphrey,' she called as she left.

I was HAPPY-HAPPY-HAPPY about what had just happened. I realized that I hadn't seen everyone in the family all together in one room so far.

I crossed my toes and hoped my Plan would work.

I don't know how long it takes to eat pizza, but I took a chance and jiggled the lock-that-doesn't-lock on my cage.

The table my cage was on had a smooth leg to slide down. I scurried over to the doll's house, and went into the living room.

I looked at the TV, trying to imagine what it would be like to live in a hamster-sized house with my own television. Is there a hamster channel?

This time, I tried the little chair but it was too small – even for a hamster.

Then I darted into the kitchen, hoping for some more fried chicken and mashed potatoes.

I opened the little fridge, but there was nothing inside.

I climbed the stairs and entered the second bedroom. I'd missed that the first time.

It had windows that went to the floor and they opened on to a little balcony.

It was fun to stand there, but then I had to check out the bed.

Aaah. It was such a nice bed with four tall columns and a little cover over the top.

It was almost as if it had been made for me.

I lay down and thought about how soft it was. And how cosy it was.

And then . . . I think maybe I dozed off!

The next thing I knew, Sophie was standing by my cage with a piece of pizza in one hand. It smelled hamster-licious!

'Hi, Humphrey,' she said. 'I'm sorry you can't eat pizza because it's delicious. But Timothy started screaming and Mum and Dad both left the room. They haven't come back yet, so I thought I'd talk to you.'

She sat down on her bed and stared into my cage.

'It was nice for a while,' she said in a soft voice.

I didn't squeak a word because *I wasn't in my cage*!

I hoped this risk was worth it.

Suddenly Sophie said, 'Humphrey? Where are you? Are you playing hide-and-seek?'

Again, I didn't answer. So she stood up and opened the cage door.

(I'd closed it behind me so she had no idea I wasn't there.)

Sophie poked around in my bedding. Then she peeked into my sleeping hut.

'Humphrey? HUMPHREY!' she cried.

I didn't move a muscle.

She raced to the door.

'Humphrey's gone!' she wailed.

(I could tell that she and Timothy were related, but Sophie was even louder.)

'Help me!' she cried.

In seconds, Mr and Mrs Kaminski appeared.

'What's wrong? Are you all right?' Sophie's father asked.

Sophie started crying. 'Humphrey's . . . not . . . in . . . his . . . cage!' she said between sobs. 'He's gone!'

Mr Kaminski rushed to my cage and started

feeling around in the bedding.

'Where could he be?' he asked. 'Was the cage door open?'

'Nooooo,' Sophie cried. 'It was closed!'

I hated to see her cry, but at least she and her parents were in the same room.

Mr Kaminski looked up from my cage. 'He's not here.'

'He must be here somewhere,' Sophie's mum said. 'Let's look around.'

So the family looked up and down, high and low . . . but it was a LONG-LONG-LONG time before they looked in the doll's house.

'He's gone! Humphrey's gone!' Sophie howled. 'And it's all my fault! Everyone in class will be furious with me! Even Mrs Brisbane!'

Her father tried to calm her down.

Between her tears, Sophie explained that after she'd put me in the doll's house and I'd gone in the kitchen, the bath and the bed, she'd closed the cage door so carefully.

Mrs Kaminski came over to the little house, leaned down – and that was it! She started to laugh. I hadn't heard her laugh before.

'Humphrey's having a nice little nap right

here,' she said. 'Come on, Sophie. Look.'

Sophie rushed over and her wails turned to giggles.

'Oh, Humphrey!' she said. 'I thought you'd run away. Everyone in Room 26 would be upset. And I'd be upset!'

She started to cry again.

'It's all right.' Her dad patted her shoulder.

'How did he get out?' she asked.

'I've heard hamsters are pretty good at escaping from their cages,' Mr Kaminski said.

He was right about that!

Sophie picked me up and then it happened.

'Waaah! Waaah! WAAAH!'

'I'll get him,' Mrs Kaminski said.

'Let him cry for a bit,' Mr Kaminski said.

'I think I should check on him,' Sophie's mum said, heading towards the door.

'All you care about is Timothy! You don't ever want to talk to me! You don't even care about Humphrey!' she cried.

Sophie had me cupped in her hand, but I could see the look on her mother's face.

'Oh, Sophie! You know how much we love you!' she said.

'You're our first baby,' her dad said. 'And we couldn't love you more!'

They both hugged Sophie while Timothy screamed in the background.

'Timothy's having some problems,' Mrs Kaminski said. 'But he'll be better soon.'

'I'll go and get him,' Mr Kaminski said.

Sophie's mum smiled. 'I have a better idea. Sophie, why don't you get Timothy and bring him here? After all, you're his big sister. You know how to pick him up carefully.'

Sophie wiped away her tears. 'All right.'

Mr Kaminski gently put me back in my cage and closed the door. He checked the lock and said, 'It's latched tightly.'

Humans always think that, thank goodness.

Sophie returned a minute later, carrying the crying blanket. At least the crying was softer now.

'Look, Timothy,' Sophie said. 'This is Humphrey the hamster.'

She walked over to the cage and held the blanket up.

I thought quickly and hopped on my wheel.

'Hi, Timothy,' I squeaked. 'Watch me spin on my wheel!'

And then, the most amazing thing happened. Timothy stopped crying and stared at me, so I kept spinning.

'Isn't he cute, Timothy?' Sophie asked.

Timothy actually smiled!

'Look, Humphrey! He likes you!' Sophie said.

Mr and Mrs Kaminski began to laugh.

'Goo,' Timothy said.

I'm not sure what that meant, but I'm pretty sure it meant he liked me.

'GOO-GOO-GOO!' I squeaked and Timothy giggled.

'That's his first laugh in days,' his mum said. 'He must be feeling better!'

I was feeling better, too. Being caught out of my cage was risky, but I was HAPPY-HAPPY-HAPPY to help the Kaminskis get together – even Timothy.

I finally got tired of spinning and climbed up my ladder.

Sophie handed Timothy to her dad and they all sat on the bed, next to my cage.

'I'm so sorry I haven't had time for you,' her mum said. 'Timothy is so lucky to have you as a sister.'

'We're all lucky to have Sophie,' her dad said.

'YES-YES-YES!' I squeaked and they all laughed.

'GOO-GOO-GOO!' Timothy gurgled and everyone laughed again.

'How did your homework go?' Mr Kaminski asked.

Sophie read them her paragraph about the Island of the Parrots and they loved it.

'You know, we *are* a family,' Sophie's mother said. 'Let's start acting like one.'

Then they talked about setting up a schedule where they'd have time to listen to Sophie and time for Timothy and time for Mr Kaminski's reports.

They kept talking, but I didn't hear it all.

I'd done everything I could do as a classroom pet.

But to squeak the truth – I needed some rest!

My Writer's Ramblings

It isn't always easy
To be a classroom pet,
But what I did at Sophie's house
May be my best trick yet!

Pearl

I was happy to get back to Room 26 on Monday and even happier to know that I'd helped Sophie out. I always like to lend a helping paw.

Mrs Brisbane asked how the weekend had gone.

'Oh, it was wonderful,' Sophie said. 'You should have seen Humphrey in my doll's house! He got in the bath and on the bed, just like it was his own little house.'

It would have been nice to have a real house, but I was happy to be in my cage and back in Room 26.

I had my schedule for Monday all worked out: maths, nap, English, nap, lunch, nap, break, nap, science, reading and NAP! I even dozed while my friends came into Room 26 that morning.

But my schedule didn't work out because Mrs Brisbane started the day with the announcement that we had a special guest.

I raced to the front of my cage, but all I saw were my usual Room 26 classmates.

'Nicole, would you like to introduce our guest?' Mrs Brisbane asked.

'Now?' Nicole said.

Mrs Brisbane nodded. 'I'll get her.'

She disappeared into the cloakroom and then came out carrying a large tank.

'This is Pearl,' Nicole said. 'Mrs Brisbane said I could bring her so you'd see what a real dragon looks like.'

There was quite a bit of commotion among my friends as you can imagine!

'I'll put Pearl's cage on the table next to Humphrey,' Mrs Brisbane said. 'Then everybody can come up and take a look at her.'

'Eeek!' I squeaked. 'Can't you put her somewhere else?'

Mrs Brisbane was already walking over to our table.

'I'll put her right between Humphrey and Og so they can both see her,' she said.

I was curious about Pearl, but I wasn't sure whether I really wanted to meet a dragon.

She was much smaller than dragons in books. Even so, she might be able to breathe fire!

When I could actually see her, I was *certain* I didn't want to meet a dragon.

My whiskers wiggled and my tail twitched, but I couldn't squeak a word.

Pearl was quite small for a dragon but huge compared to me.

Her head was shaped flat on top with spines all over it. She had large, ugly claws, and she was all kinds of colours, from green to pink.

She looked right at me and stuck out her tongue, which is REALLY-REALLY-REALLY rude!

'She's so pretty!' Kelsey said.

Maybe Kelsey needed glasses.

I don't think Og liked Pearl either. He started hopping around his tank and twanging, 'BOING-BOING-BOING!'

I climbed up to the tippy-top of my cage so I could get a better look.

'BOING-BOING-BOING-BOING!' Og continued.

Then, Pearl *hissed*. Even over all of Og's noise, I could hear her.

'Hisssssss!'

I didn't think that was a friendly thing to do, since Og and I live in Room 26 and she was just a visitor. But I kept quiet. I didn't want her to hiss at me.

Meanwhile, my classmates pointed and pushed and tried to get a better look at Pearl.

'She looks like a dinosaur,' Sophie said.

'She looks like a dragon,' Harry said.

'She's actually a reptile,' Nicole explained. 'A lizard.'

'Wow!' Thomas said. 'We have a reptile, a rodent and an amphibian in our class – and we're all mammals!'

'Rodents are mammals too, Thomas!' I squeaked.

Mrs Brisbane laughed. 'Very good, Thomas. But now you need to return to your seats and begin class.'

My friends all moved to their tables.

Pearl stayed right where she was.

'Hi, Pearl,' I squeaked, though my voice was shaky. 'I'm Humphrey. Welcome to Room 26.'

Pearl turned her head a little. 'Hissssss!'

No manners at all! The dragon in the book was much nicer!

'BOING-BOING-BOING!' Og was so excited he did a high dive into the water side of his tank.

I swallowed hard. If Pearl was going to be next to me all day, I REALLY-REALLY-REALLY wanted to make friends with her. At least I didn't want to be her enemy!

I tried to be calm as I looked over at her tank. It had rocks, leaves, a water dish – even a thermometer, which was something Og and I don't have.

'Nice tank!' I squeaked.

Pearl turned her head from side to side and then she did it again!

'Hissssssss!' she said.

I was pretty sure Pearl didn't like me.

How could anybody dislike a friendly classroom pet like me?

I guess Og was on my side, because he left

the water side of his tank and said, 'BOING-BOING-SCREEE!'

'SCREEE' is a sound he makes only when he thinks there's danger around.

'Calm down,' I told him. 'Maybe she's scared of *us*!'

I guess Og had never thought of that, because he was quiet for a long time.

'Let's listen to Mrs Brisbane,' I said. 'She's our friend.'

Pearl, Og and I were totally silent for a while.

There wasn't a squeak, a BOING, *or* a hiss, which was good, because Mrs Brisbane had something important to say.

'You've written a couple of paragraphs about what you'd do if you could fly,' she said. 'And you're doing a good job. Now I want you to turn your ideas into a story. Instead of writing about what you would do if you could fly, I'd like you to take those same ideas and write a story as if you already *can* fly.'

My friends looked as puzzled as I was.

'Instead of saying, "If I could fly like a bumblebee, I'd fly to the top of a mountain," write it as if you *are* a bumblebee and describe

what the world looks like through your eyes,'
she said. 'In other words, turn it into fiction.'

My friends looked unsqueakably puzzled,
but Mrs Brisbane helped them, one by one.

During break, Pearl, Og and I stayed on our
best behaviour.

I was beginning to think dragons weren't so
bad, after all.

But I changed my mind later in the day,
when my friends were at lunch.

I decided to take a chance and get a closer
look at Pearl.

I jiggled my lock-that-doesn't-lock and the
cage door opened.

I quietly tiptoed over to Pearl's tank.

To squeak the truth, up close, she was even
larger and more terrifying than I'd thought.
Those spines looked sharp and she had a large
tongue which she stuck out at me . . . again!

I'm pretty brave for a small creature, so I
crossed my toes for luck and tiptoed closer.
(But I wished I had a magic shield, like Gil
Goodfriend.)

'Welcome to Room 26, Pearl,' I said. 'We're so happy to have you . . .'

Pearl's neck puffed up and she said, 'Hissssss' even louder than before!

I backed up all the way to my cage.

'Never mind!' I squeaked as I pulled the door shut behind me.

·ö·

At the end of the day, Mrs Brisbane read us the last chapter of the dragon book by Cameron Cole.

It was SAD-SAD-SAD when Gil Goodfriend said goodbye to Goldie and the other dragons. But at least they got to go on a picnic on a beautiful, sunny day.

I looked over at Pearl and saw her tail twitching.

At the end of the book, there was a hint that Gil and the dragon would meet again, which made me very happy.

But if Goldie had been as unfriendly as Pearl, I wouldn't have liked the book so much!

I was so happy when Nicole's mum came and took that tank away.

'Goodbye, Pearl! Come see us again!' I squeaked.

But when she was gone, I added, 'But not for a LONG-LONG-LONG time!'

⚬

I was tired that night, but after Aldo left, I opened my cage door again and hurried over to Og's tank.

'What do you think of Pearl?' I asked Og.

He didn't say a thing for a moment. Then he started hopping up and down, up and down. 'BOING-BOING-BOING!' he said.

'I agree,' I told him. 'She wasn't polite with all that hissing. I still think she was a little afraid of us. She's probably never seen a frog or a hamster before.'

Og turned his head left. Then he turned his head right.

I imagine he was thinking.

'BOING!' he shouted. He sounded cheerful.

'Think of it, Og,' I answered. 'A dragon was afraid of us! Or maybe she was a little jealous because we get to be classroom pets and she doesn't.'

For a second, I was sorry for Pearl. But that didn't last long.

I still had work to do, so I went back to my cage and grabbed my little notebook.

Despite the fact that I was tired, I knew I was behind the rest of the class and I had to catch up! I looked at my list of things I'd like to do.

- Help Holly visit Phoebe
- Help Mrs Brisbane visit her son Jason in Japan
- Help Joey see more of his dad
- Help Cassie go to the seaside
- Help Sophie go to the parrot island
- Help Simon go to Italy
- Help Kelsey go to the ballet
- Help Daniel meet D. D. Denby

Reading the list, I realized that what I REALLY-REALLY-REALLY like to do is to help my human friends. There was no way one little hamster could accomplish such big goals in real life, but Mrs Brisbane said it should be fiction. Maybe if I used my imagination, I could think of something.

'Watch out,' I squeaked to Og. 'There might be another brainstorm!'

If I could fly, how could I help my friends? A flying squirrel wouldn't work for me. I'd need to fly like a hamster.

But one hamster couldn't accomplish everything I wanted to do.

I'd need my own great big aeroplane. Then I could fly to the Pyramids and Phoebe's house and I could fly Mrs Brisbane to Tokyo.

That was it! Flying Hamster Airlines! I could fly all my friends to places they wanted to go to. And since it was an imaginary airline, I could fly to imaginary places, too!

'Og, if I could fly, I'd start my own airline,' I squeaked.

He splashed around in the water, which usually means he's happy.

But I don't know if frogs even know what an airline *is*.

'That means you fly people all over the world in a big shiny aeroplane,' I explained. 'Hey, if you could fly, you could start a Flying Frog Airlines!'

'BOING-BOING-BOING-BOING!' Og

leaped into the water and began to splash.

I guess he knew what an airline was after all.

I grabbed my pencil and began to write.

I'm proud to be the first hamster
ever to become an aeroplane pilot.
Now that I've started my own
company, Flying Hamster Airlines, I
can fly my human friends anywhere
they want to go.

I kept on writing, without even pausing.

First, I'll drop Holly off at
Phoebe's house, and spend some time
catching up with my old friend.
Next, I'll take Joey to the town
where his dad lives. Then I'll zip
over to Europe so Simon can eat
Italian food and I'll take Kelsey to
see a ballet in Paris . . .

I wrote and wrote and wrote.

I didn't even notice how tired my paw was
getting.

And when I was finished and I read what I'd written, I felt . . . well, proud!

My Writer's Ramblings

I tried and tried again
And then I kept on trying.
And now I am so happy:
My imagination's flying!

Rosie's Casa

My friends' imaginations were flying as well – all except for Joey's.

He still spent more time staring at his notebook than writing in it.

Believe me, I knew how he felt.

Mrs Brisbane was encouraging, but somehow, she wasn't getting through to him.

One day, the Most Important Person at Longfellow School – our headmaster Mr Morales – came in to see how we were doing.

'I hear you have a room full of authors here,' he said. 'Mrs Brisbane said you're doing very well.'

He was wearing a tie with little pencils all over it.

He wandered up and down the aisles, looking at each notebook and making comments.

When he read Small-Paul's page about time-travelling through space, he said, 'Fantastic idea!'

He high-fived Sophie when he read about the parrots.

He had something nice to say about everyone. Then he came to Joey.

'So, what are you writing about?' the headmaster asked. He couldn't really tell, because Joey had covered his page with his arm.

'I'm off to a slow start,' Joey said.

Mr Morales persuaded him to move his arm. He studied Joey's page. 'Keep going. I love your idea of flying to Africa.'

Joey muttered, 'Thanks.' I don't think he believed Mr Morales, but our headmaster would never lie!

'What's this?' Mr Morales asked, nudging Joey's arm. 'On this page?'

Joey wrinkled his nose. 'Oh, just doodles. I'm always doodling.'

'But they're very good,' Mr Morales said.

'They are very, very good.'

'I like to fool around with drawing,' Joey said, sitting up straighter in his chair.

'You should illustrate your story,' Mr Morales said. 'Don't you think so, Mrs Brisbane?'

Mrs Brisbane came over to Joey's desk and looked at his notebook. 'I hadn't seen these. Mr Morales is right.'

'Is it all right for us to draw pictures for our stories?' Thomas asked.

'Yes,' Mrs Brisbane said. 'I think it would be great. But this *is* a writing assignment so you need to have words to go with the pictures.'

Joey seemed more interested.

Mr Morales looked at Rosie's notebook next. He smiled when he read what she'd written. 'Great description.'

Rosie's smile lit up the whole room!

Then he talked to the whole class. 'Mrs Brisbane and I have been talking, and we've come up with a big surprise for you when you've finished your stories.'

That got my whiskers wiggling! And my friends seemed excited, too.

'So do the best work you can,' Mr Morales

continued. 'You've got something big to look forward to.'

'How big?' I squeaked. 'As big as an elephant? Or a dragon?'

Mr Morales heard me and laughed. 'Oh, do you have a story idea, Humphrey?'

'Yes! I do!' I squeaked.

Everybody laughed at that. 'I think I'd like to read your story,' Mr Morales said, acting as if he understood me.

Suddenly, I realized that as good as my story might be, no one would ever read it.

And stories are meant to be shared.

I hopped on my wheel and began to spin to shake off my disappointment.

As soon as school emptied out, I scurried out of Room 26. 'I'll be quick,' I told Og.

'BOING-BOING!' Og chimed.

As soon as I slid under the door of Room 12, Gigi said, 'Is that you, Humphrey?'

'Yes, here I am!' I squeaked as I rushed towards her table.

I swung up to her table top and noticed that

she wasn't shaking the way she usually did.

'What's new?' I asked.

'Yesterday, a boy told me I was his best friend,' she squeaked in her soft voice. 'And today, a girl said she loves me!'

'That is unsqueakably wonderful!' I said. 'That's why being a classroom pet is the BEST-BEST-BEST job in the world.'

'Now I understand,' she said. 'Thank you for encouraging me.'

'Any time,' I said.

I could see it was getting dark outside.

'I've got to get back,' I told Gigi. 'But I'll see you soon!'

When I returned, I told Og, 'Now Gigi loves being a classroom pet.'

'BOING-BOING!' Og replied. I knew he loved being a classroom pet, too. Especially in Room 26.

I worked on my story, even though I knew no one else would ever read it.

Still, it was exciting to get my ideas down on paper.

On Thursday morning, I overheard Joey talking to Mrs Brisbane.

'So, what did your mum say?' our teacher asked him.

Joey looked so disappointed. 'She said this isn't a good week. That's what she says every week. I don't think I'll ever get a turn.'

'Your mother is very busy. But I have an idea,' our teacher said. 'Rosie said she could take Humphrey home this weekend. Don't you live on her street?'

Joey nodded.

'It's her first time taking Humphrey home,' Mrs Brisbane said. 'Maybe you could go to her house and help her out.'

Joey shrugged. 'I guess I could do that.'

That afternoon, I overheard Mrs Brisbane talking to Rolling-Rosie.

'I was wondering if you'd like to invite Joey to come over this weekend,' Mrs Brisbane said. 'He hasn't been able to take Humphrey home and he knows a lot about hamsters.'

'Sure,' Rosie said. 'I'd like that. He lives just down the street.'

Mrs Brisbane hesitated. 'And you know,

maybe you could help Joey with his writing. He has wonderful ideas, but he has trouble getting them down on paper. You're doing a great job, so maybe . . .'

Rosie nodded. 'Yes, I'll do it.'

'But don't let him think you don't like what he's written,' Mrs Brisbane said.

Rosie shook her head. 'No! I'll just cheer him on. Like you always do.'

'Thank you, Rosie,' Mrs Brisbane told her with a smile.

On Friday, Rosie's dad – she called him 'Papa' – came to pick us up.

'So, Humphrey, I hope you know what you're getting into, coming to our house,' Papa said. 'It's a pretty busy place.'

'I know I'll like it,' I said.

When we got there, I met her younger brother and sister, Diego and Elena. And Rosie's mum – she called her 'Mama' – was very friendly.

'Rosie is in charge of Humphrey,' she told Diego and Elena. 'Don't touch the cage or do anything else without asking her first.'

She is a wise mama!

On Saturday, Mama went to the shops. When the doorbell rang, Rosie rolled to the door as her father opened it.

Joey was standing there, holding a skateboard.

'Come on in,' Papa said in his booming voice.

'Here's Humphrey,' she said as she rolled her chair in my direction. 'I waited for you to clean out his cage. I could use your help.'

Joey leaned down and put his face close to mine.

'Hey, Humph,' he said. 'How's it going?'

'GREAT-GREAT-GREAT,' I squeaked.

'Make yourself at home,' Papa said. '*Mi casa es su casa.*'

'Thanks,' Joey said, putting his skateboard and backpack on the floor next to the table.

'I'm glad you remembered your skateboard,' Rosie said.

'Why'd you ask me to bring it?' Joey asked. 'And my notebook?'

Rosie's eyes were sparkling. 'The skateboard, because it's nice outside. And the notebook, because . . . well, you'll see.'

Just then, Diego chased Elena through the room.

'Whoa!' Rosie's father said. 'Stop and say hello to Joey.'

'Hi, Joey,' Diego said.

Elena giggled.

'Hi,' Joey said.

'Now you're it,' Diego said to Elena and she chased him out of the room, squealing with laughter.

Papa shook his head. 'Those two. Do you have any brothers or sisters?'

Joey shook his head. 'No. It's just me. And my dog, Skipper.'

Thinking about Skipper made me glad I didn't get to go to Joey's house after all.

Rosie and Joey got busy cleaning my cage, with Papa's help.

First, Rosie took me out of the cage. She held me in one hand and gently stroked my back with one finger. It felt like a gentle breeze on my fur and I shivered with delight.

Rosie put me in my hamster ball and set me on the floor.

When I started to roll, Papa chuckled. 'Look

at him go!'

They put my bedding in a bag and cleaned almost everything in my cage with warm, soapy water.

I was HAPPY-HAPPY-HAPPY they didn't move my mirror and find my notebook. I don't think warm, soapy water would do it much good. I was glad they didn't wash *me* in warm, soapy water, too. (Hamsters should never get wet.)

When everything was dry, Rosie filled the base of my cage with fresh bedding.

She remembered to mix a little of my old bedding in with it before Joey slid it back into place.

Then they put all my things back, too.

Papa filled my water bottle and Joey put some food in my dish.

'Humphrey, I think it's time to move you back into your house,' Rosie said.

I sniffed here and I sniffed there. It smelled fresh and familiar all at the same time.

I was so happy, I hopped on my wheel and started spinning.

Joey and Rosie went off to wash their hands

again. When they came back, they watched me.

'How's your story coming along?' Rosie asked.

Joey shrugged. 'Not so great. I sure can't write like Cameron Cole and that great dragon story. Mrs Brisbane wants me to make it more descriptive, but I don't know what to write. How about you?'

'I don't know,' Rosie said. 'I think mine's going well. Want to hear it?'

Joey wanted to hear it and so did I.

'One day, I turned into a graceful bird and rose up out of my chair, high into the air,' she began. 'Against the blue sky, I felt the wind in my feathers and saw the green earth below. As fast as my wings would carry me, I flew above the Nile River and then to the Egyptian desert, where the Great Pyramids and the Great Sphinx stand. I landed right on top of the statue of the Sphinx, which has the body of a lion but a human head. I looked down at the statue and said, "I'm sorry for you, Sphinx. You are stuck in the sand and can't travel. But I have wings and I can fly!"'

For a moment, I felt like a bird landing on the Sphinx!

'That's really good,' Joey said. 'That's *great*. Mine is nothing like that.'

'Would you like to read it?' Rosie asked. 'Maybe I could help.'

'I don't think anything would help me,' he said. 'I don't have an imagination.'

Rosie smiled. 'Everybody has imagination! Come on, read it to me.'

Joey slowly opened his backpack and took out his notebook. 'I'll read it,' he said. 'But it's no good.'

I HOPED-HOPED-HOPED he was wrong.

Joey began to read. 'I flew like a hawk to Africa and saw animals in the wild. I saw elephants, giraffes, lions, rhinos and monkeys. I especially liked the elephants. They were amazing.'

He lowered his notebook. 'That's it. Pretty bad, isn't it?'

Rosie shook her head. 'It's not bad. You just need to put some *zing* into it.'

'*Zing*? What's that?' Joey asked.

I'd never heard of *zing*, either, but I thought my writing could use some!

'It's like cooking dinner,' Rosie explained.

'Mama puts in the meat and the potatoes and the vegetables and then she spices them up. Pepper, salt, garlic, hot sauce. That's the *zing*.'

I don't know about Joey, but I was suddenly hungry!

'I don't get it,' he said. 'Can you show me?'

Rosie thought for a moment.

'Well, you told me what you saw. But you need to make me see it, too,' Rosie said.

'Oh, I can see it,' Joey said. 'I see a monkey in a tree.'

'Doing what?' Rosie asked.

Joey was silent for a long time. A little too long, I thought.

I knew what monkeys did. I saw them in a video in the library. (Sometimes at night, I sneak into the library to read and watch videos.)

I scrambled up the side of my cage, and took a giant leap on to my tree branch. I hung there from one paw and bounced up and down.

'SQUEAK-SQUEAK-SQUEAK!' I said, trying to sound like a monkey.

Rosie saw me first and giggled. 'Look! Humphrey's acting like a monkey.'

Joey leaned in and watched me, so I swung

from the branch to my ladder and climbed it to the tippy-top of my cage. I hung there by one paw, swinging back and forth.

'He *is* like a monkey, swinging from branch to branch,' Joey said.

He bent over his notebook and started scribbling.

'Here's the monkey,' he said as he held up the page for Rosie to see.

I could see it, too. It was an unsqueakably great drawing of a monkey swinging from a tree.

Rosie's eyes opened wide. 'That's great! I can almost see him moving. Can you write the words to describe it?'

Joey thought for a bit and then he wrote, 'The playful monkeys swing from branch to branch.'

Rosie clapped her hands. 'What else would you see?'

Joey stared at the page and then he said, 'What about a lion?'

Oh, dear. Hamsters aren't like lions at all. But I thought about the video.

I raced up to the side of the cage, faced Joey and said, 'ROAR!'

I tried my best, but I know it sounded like a great big 'SQUEAK!'

'Ha-ha,' Joey laughed. 'Humphrey's roaring like a lion!'

And he started scribbling again.

'Humphrey's so funny! It's like he understands you,' Rosie said.

When he showed Rosie the drawing, she clapped her hands again. 'You're a great artist!' she said. 'Can you describe what you drew?'

Joey thought for a long time, but then he wrote something down.

Joey stared at his notebook again. 'Maybe there would be . . . a rhino?'

'Rhino?' I squeaked. 'I've got it.'

I scurried to one side of my cage and then lowered my head and ran as fast as I could to the other side of the cage. 'Charge!' I squeaked.

Joey chuckled and quickly wrote something down.

'What about elephants and giraffes?' Rosie asked.

Small furry hamsters have nothing in common with elephants and giraffes. I was thinking about how to help Joey, but it turns out he didn't need my help.

'I know what to do,' he said as he wrote.

Whew! That was a HUGE-HUGE-HUGE relief.

Joey wrote and wrote and wrote some more. At last, he was finished.

'How's this?' he asked. Then he read from his notebook. 'With the eyes and the speed of a hawk, I flew to Africa and saw amazing animals in the wild. I watched the playful monkeys, swinging from branch to branch. Then I saw a mighty lion and heard its powerful roar. From a safe place, I watched a rhino charge with its great, sharp horn and a giraffe eating leaves from the top of a tree. My favourite part was seeing elephants in the wild and hearing their loud trumpeting. I decided to stay in Africa and never come back.'

Rosie clapped loudly. 'That was great! It has loads of *zing*!'

I couldn't clap my paws, but I squeaked, 'Good job, Joey!' at the top of my tiny lungs.

'Just one thing,' Rosie said. 'I think you need a descriptive word in front of "hawk". Mrs Brisbane asked for that.'

'Oh,' Joey said. 'How do you spell "magnificent"?'

Rosie helped him out and Joey wrote it down.

'Tomorrow, I'm going to illustrate the whole thing,' he said. 'That's the fun part.'

Both of them were smiling happily. I think I was smiling, too.

'What do we do next?' Joey asked. 'I don't have to be home for a while.'

Before I knew it, we were all heading outside. I was in my hamster ball, sitting on Rosie's lap.

Joey pulled his helmet and knee pads out of his backpack as he followed with his skateboard.

There were orange cones down the middle of Rosie's driveway, but they weren't in a straight line.

'It's an obstacle course,' Rosie said. 'You can try it on your skateboard. I'll try it in my wheelchair. And Humphrey can try it in his hamster ball.'

'Great!' Joey sounded really excited.

'Great!' I squeaked, because I LOVE-LOVE-LOVE obstacle courses.

First, Joey zoomed down the driveway,

weaving between the orange cones.

At the very end, he managed to do a 'wheelie', which means the front wheels of the skateboard lifted up off the ground.

'Way to go!' Rosie gave Joey a high-five.

Her turn was next. Rosie wheeled between the cones, without knocking any of them over, just like Joey. She may not have wings, but she made that wheelchair fly!

And just like Joey, she managed to pop a wheelie on the rear wheels of her chair.

'That was amazing!' Joey said, giving Rosie a high-five. 'Now it's Humphrey's turn.'

Joey picked up my hamster ball and set it at the end of the driveway.

'Go, Humphrey!' Rosie and Joey shouted.

I think a skateboard and a wheelchair are easier to control than a hamster ball. I managed to get around the first cone, but I got stuck when I ran straight into the second cone.

'That's okay, Humphrey,' Joey said, as he moved my hamster ball away from the cone.

I decided to forget about the cones. I starting running in a straight line.

My hamster ball picked up speed.

'That's the way, Humphrey!' I heard Rosie shout.

Then I heard something else. 'He's going to roll into the street!' Rosie shrieked.

'Eeek!' I shouted. I don't think anyone could hear me from inside the hamster ball.

I heard a loud RATTLE-RATTLE-RATTLE coming up behind me and my hamster ball came to a sudden stop.

'It's okay, Humphrey,' Joey said. 'You're safe.'

Joey had skateboarded down the driveway and stopped me just in time.

I hate to think what might have happened if I'd ended up in the street!

'Thanks, Joey,' I said.

'Thanks, Joey,' Rosie said as she wheeled her chair next to us.

Joey picked me up and handed the hamster ball to Rosie.

She opened the top and smiled at me.

'You did a great job, Humphrey,' she said. 'But you *didn't* pop a wheelie.'

How could I have? My hamster ball has no wheels.

But it was still a great day. I was pawsitively

happy that Joey's story was better. And Joey and Rosie had tons more fun making up new obstacle courses – using their imaginations!

My Writer's Ramblings

I'd like to pop a wheelie
Almost more than anything,
But I was very happy,
To help Joey's writing 'zing'.

Special Guest

'Og, Joey's story is great! Rosie helped him a lot, and I helped a little, too!' I squeaked to my neighbour when I returned on Monday morning.

'BOING!' Og twanged with excitement.

The rest of the week was BUSY-BUSY-BUSY as my friends finished writing their stories and illustrating them as well. They worked on special paper and made them into little books.

At night, I finished my story and tried to add lots of zing. I was pleased when I could write: 'The End'.

'When is our special surprise?' Cassie asked one day. 'Is it a person, place or thing? And what are we supposed to do?'

'Calm-Down-Cassie,' Mrs Brisbane said.

'The surprise is on Friday and all you have to do is show up.'

Cassie looked calmer after she said that.

Once the stories were finished on Thursday, Mrs Brisbane placed all the notebooks on the table where Og's tank and my cage sit.

Wow! They looked unsqueakably wonderful! They had illustrations and fantastic covers and everything!

I guess my story was a little plain, but at least I'd finished it.

Later that night, when Aldo came in to clean, he saw the finished books.

'What's this?' he asked. 'Your class wrote books?'

'Yes,' I squeaked. 'Do you like them?'

Aldo began to thumb through the books. 'These are really good,' he said. 'Leave it to Mrs Brisbane to teach her students to write so well.'

Aldo looked through a few more. 'When I get to be a teacher, I want my students to write like this,' he said.

Then he looked right at me. 'And Humphrey, I *am* going to be a teacher before long! A very good teacher, I hope.'

'I know you will!' I squeaked.

Aldo is so good at sweeping and dusting and going to school and being a friend . . . I'm sure he'll be a GREAT-GREAT-GREAT teacher, too.

Later, while he dusted Mrs Brisbane's desk, he said, 'Well, what do you know?'

He was looking at a piece of paper. 'I'd like to be here for this,' he said. 'I don't have class then. I'll ask Mrs Brisbane if I can come.'

'Come to WHAT?' I squeaked, but he didn't answer.

I was happy that Aldo was coming to our class.

I wasn't happy that I didn't know what the surprise was!

Once Aldo was gone, I had two things on my mind – getting a good look at all of the books and finding out what that note said.

I jiggled my lock-that-doesn't-lock and opened the door.

Then I strolled along the table, looking at each book lined up there.

'Oh!' I exclaimed when I saw Sophie's book.

The parrots looked colourful, but their sharp beaks looked a little frightening.

'Gee!' I said as I looked at Small-Paul's book. His time-travel machine was awe-inspiring and the adventure he wrote about was exciting and even a little scary.

Kelsey's book was all pink and purple and she did a wonderful job of describing a ballet. And to think that Be-Careful-Kelsey once thought she was clumsy!

Simon's book about Italy made me a little bit hungry. Luckily, I had some celery stored in my cheek pouch.

When I got to Joey's book, all I could say was, 'Wow!' His descriptions of the animals in Africa were fantastic, but his drawings were like something out of a library book. Yet I knew they'd come from his own brain.

'Og, Joey is very talented!' I squeaked.

'BOING!' Og agreed before making a spectacular leap into the water.

My friends had done something wonderful! They'd become writers.

It was a lot of work, but their books were beautiful.

All that reading made me tired and I knew it would be a lot of work to climb up Mrs Brisbane's desk.

I decided not to go. It would be fun to find out about the surprise at the same time as my classmates.

When I returned to my cage, I took out the little notebook from behind my mirror.

I knew my story wasn't as great as the ones my classmates had written. And I knew none of my friends would ever know I had written a story.

But when I read about the Flying Hamster Airlines, I could picture myself flying all my friends to the places they loved most.

And I felt a special feeling. I think it's called 'joy'.

The next day, everyone in Room 26 was jittery and excited, because we knew we were going to have a special surprise.

I didn't want the surprise to be the return of Pearl!

I didn't want the surprise to be something

terrible, such as Mrs Brisbane leaving!

I did want the surprise to be something wonderful. And it was.

After morning break, strange things started to happen.

First, Mr Morales came into Room 26. He doesn't come here too often, because he has so much to do as headmaster of the school.

Next, my dear friend Ms Mac entered with her entire first grade class.

And the biggest surprise was that she brought Gigi with her!

'I think it's time for Humphrey and Og to meet our class guinea pig,' she said as she set Gigi between Og's tank and my cage.

Of course, Gigi and I had already met, but Ms Mac didn't know that.

'Gigi, meet Og,' I said. 'Og, meet Gigi.'

'BOING! BOING! BOING!' Og hopped around his tank.

'Nice to meet you, too,' Gigi squealed.

'I knew you'd like each other,' I squeaked happily.

Once the students from Room 12 were seated, Mr Morales came to the front of the room.

'Boys and girls, I know you've been working hard on your writing,' he said. 'And you've done a very good job. So we have a special guest today.'

I turned to the back of the room, where a tall woman with red hair stood next to Mrs Brisbane. And surprise – Aldo was there, too!

Mr Morales continued. 'I want you to make her feel welcome and to listen and treat her with respect. Here she is, the author Cameron Cole.'

As the tall woman walked to the front of the room, my classmates all applauded. They looked as excited and amazed as I was.

First of all, I'd thought Cameron Cole was a man.

Second of all, I never thought I'd meet the author of the dragon book in person!

Once the clapping and cheering stopped, Ms Cole began to answer students' questions.

I climbed up to the tippy-top of my cage so I had a good view.

'I like to write stories, because I like to use my imagination,' she said. 'Does anyone here like that, too?'

Every hand – plus my paw – went up.

She pulled a bright blue notebook out of her bag. 'It's important to keep a notebook,' she said. 'I take my notebook everywhere.'

Mrs Brisbane asked our class to hold up their notebooks.

I was tempted to pull mine out of its hiding place, but in the end, I left it there.

Cameron Cole continued answering questions about dragons.

No, she had never seen one, but she wasn't sure whether or not they were real.

Yes, she had seen a bearded dragon. But she hadn't seen a huge, flying, fire-breathing dragon like Goldie.

Yes, she'd loved fairy tales and dragon books when she was growing up.

Then she answered questions about writing.

Holly asked her where she got her ideas. That's what I wanted to know, too!

Ms Cole said, 'I find them absolutely everywhere! Things that happened to me, things that happened to people I know, things I read in newspapers and books, conversations I overhear. You need to be open to ideas and you'll find them.'

She paused to glance over at our table and smiled.

'I have to admit, I had an imaginary dragon friend when I was little,' she said. 'I'm very grateful to him for inspiring me. And I used to lie on the grass and look up at the clouds, imagining there was a secret kingdom with a great big castle up there. That was the beginning of the Gil Goodfriend story.'

Imaginary dragon? That's a lot like an imaginary bear named Bear! Maybe Carlos will write a book about his friend one day.

'Who knows,' she said, walking over to get a closer look at Gigi, Og and me. 'Someday I might even write a book about these adorable animals.'

'Really!' I squeaked. 'I write about us all the time!'

Cameron Cole laughed. 'This hamster seems to have a lot to say.'

'I DO-DO-DO!' I replied. I could hardly believe I was talking to a real author!

'BOING!' Og added.

'Oh, and the frog has ideas, too.' Ms Cole chuckled.

'Say something, Gigi,' I told my guinea pig friend.

But Gigi was too shy to squeak.

'Mrs Brisbane said that you started with a sentence and then a paragraph and ended up with a story,' Cameron Cole said. 'That's exactly what I do when I write a book. So congratulations!'

Then our teacher announced that it was almost time for lunch.

My friends groaned. I think they would have gladly given up lunch to keep talking with Cameron Cole.

She signed our dragon book and my friends' notebooks.

I wished I could have had her sign my notebook, too.

The time had passed so quickly! My friends left for lunch and Mrs Brisbane and Ms Mac took Cameron Cole to the teachers' lounge for lunch as well.

Aldo stayed behind to talk to us.

'Well, my friends, I don't usually see you during the day,' he said. 'But I learned the author was coming, and one of the subjects I'll have to teach is writing. She gave me a lot of ideas.'

'Me too, Aldo!' I squeaked.

'I have to start my student teaching soon. That's where you practise being a teacher in a classroom,' he said. 'So wish me luck!'

'Good luck!' I shouted.

'BOING-BOING!' Og twanged.

And Gigi even managed to softly squeal, 'Luck!'

After Aldo had cleaned that night, I took out my little notebook and read my story by the light of the street lamp outside the window.

I was a little nervous about reading it. What if I didn't like it? Would I have to start all over again?

Luckily, the story sounded pretty good to me.

So I opened my lock-that-doesn't-lock and hurried over to Og's tank.

'Would you like to hear my story?' I asked.

'BOING-BOING!' Og definitely sounded interested.

And so I began to read.

I'll never forget the day I became the first hamster airline pilot ever! I started my own company, called Flying Hamster Airlines, so I could fly my human friends anywhere they wanted to go.

First, I took Do-It-Now-Daniel to the home of his favourite author, D. D. Denby. I wished I could stay and get some writing tips, but it was time to take Felipe to the theme park. Then I flew my friend Helpful-Holly to Phoebe's house. Holly helps so many people, I was happy to help her, too.

Next, my zippy plane took Joey to the town where his dad lives. He was glad to get to spend extra time with his dad. But instead of staying in town, Joey and his dad decided to fly along with me.

We whizzed over to Europe so Simon could eat Italian food. I even had a tiny bit of real Italian pizza. Yum! Then I stopped in Paris to take Kelsey to see a ballet. The dancers were so graceful, they practically flew through the air, just like my plane!

I would have stayed in Paris, but I had to fly to Africa. First, I took Rosie to see the Pyramids in Egypt. The Sphinx was larger and fiercer than I'd imagined. Then I took Joey and his dad to another part of Africa, where we saw large and colourful creatures. The trumpeting of the elephants and the roars of the lions were sounds I'll never forget. The zebras looked like someone had taken a brush to paint them black and white. I loved the giraffes and their long necks. They were so tall, I could hardly see their heads.

Next, I flew Sophie to the Island of the Parrots. It was a noisy place, but Sophie loved talking to the birds and they loved her! I wish she could understand my squeaks the way she understands the parrots.

I dropped Cassie off on a quiet beach where she could watch the waves breaking all day long.

I saved the best part of the trip for last. I flew Mrs Brisbane and her husband to Tokyo. When they surprised their son, Jason, the look on Mrs Brisbane's face made me HAPPY-HAPPY-HAPPY.

I have lots more plans for Flying Hamster Airlines. Who knows, maybe someday I'll fly you to a special place, too!

Og was silent after I finished.

Then he leaped up in his cage and said, 'BOING-BOING-BOING-BOING,' before diving into the water side of his tank.

I think he really liked it!

And I really liked reading it to him, because stories are meant to be shared.

'I think maybe Gigi would like it, too,' I said. 'But she might be asleep by now.'

Og splashed loudly.

'It *could* be a bedtime story,' I said.

Clenching the notebook between my teeth, I slid down the table leg and headed towards Room 12.

Gigi wasn't sound asleep yet. When I asked if she'd like to hear my story, she squealed with happiness.

She squealed even more when I finished. 'How did you learn to read and write?' she asked.

'I paid attention in class,' I said. 'You should try it, too.'

'I will!' Gigi said.

Then, as I headed back to Room 26, something amazing happened.

My imagination went to work and I thought of a brand-new idea! I couldn't wait to write it in my notebook.

And that's the BEST-BEST-BEST feeling in the world!

My Writer's Ramblings

When I began my story,
I felt a little fright,
But now that I have finished,
I really love to write!

Humphrey's Top Ten Tips for Writers

1. Keep a writer's notebook to jot down your ideas or you might forget them! You don't have to keep yours hidden, the way I do. It's good to have it with you most of the time.

2. Brainstorm your story ideas by writing down all your thoughts as fast as you can for five minutes. Don't stop to judge whether it's a good idea or not. When you're finished, you may have a few good ideas (a brainshower) or a lot of GREAT-GREAT-GREAT ideas (a brain blizzard)! But really, all you need is ONE idea you really like. Write something YOU'D enjoy reading.

3. Once you have a story you like, brainstorm ideas for a setting and the characters.

4. Now you can work on the story. Your story should have a definite beginning, middle and end. (That might not be as easy as it sounds but you can do it!)

5. Start filling in the details about what is happening to your characters.

6. Add some zing to your writing by using dialogue – make sure your characters don't all sound the same.

7. The more you write the better you'll get. It takes practice, so try to write on a regular basis. The more you read, the better your writing will be. Read a lot of different kinds of books, too!

8. When you're writing a story, you shouldn't think about what other people will think of it or whether it will get published. You should only think about making it the best story you can possibly write. That's all that counts.

9. REVISE-REVISE-REVISE. Each time you go through the story, you have an opportunity to make it better and better. (Cameron Cole said that professional writers revise a lot and I believe her!)

10. Don't forget that writing is fun! Write something that makes you happy, something you'd like to read, that tells a story only you can tell. Then, my friend, you will realize that writing is really fun!

Look out for my book of
unsqueakably funny jokes

Or why not try the
puzzles and games in my
fun-fun-fun activity
books?

There's one
for summer . . .

Puzzles and Games!

Humphrey's
Book of
Summer Fun

Betty G. Birney

. . . and one
for Christmas!

Humphrey and his friends have been hard at work making a brand new FUN-FUN-FUN website just for you!

Play Humphrey's exciting new game, share your pet pictures, find fun crafts and activities, read Humphrey's very own diary and discover all the latest news from your favourite furry friend at:

www.funwithhumphrey.com